SUGAR CREEK GANG
THE
SECRET HIDEOUT

Original title:
Sugar Creek Gang in School

Paul Hutchens

MOODY PRESS • CHICAGO

by PAUL HUTCHENS

ISBN 0-8024-4806-2

31 33 35 37 39 40 38 36 34 32

Printed in the United States of America

1

IF I HADN'T BEEN the janitor of our little one-room red brick schoolhouse, I don't suppose I would have cared so much when Poetry's wet, pet lamb walked around all over the floor with his muddy feet.

Lambs, you know, are not supposed to go to school, and even though the Sugar Creek Gang knew that, they thought they'd like to see what it was like to have one come in spite of the fact that it was, as a certain poem says, "against the rule."

It certainly made the children laugh and play—and it also made some of them cry and work, especially me. That is, I had to mop the floor, and I had to stay in at recess to do it, with Poetry and all the rest of the Sugar Creek Gang helping me. It took longer to get the floor clean than it should have because the lamb accidentally turned a pail of sudsy water over and it scattered itself in every direction there was.

Maybe before I tell you what the teacher said about the lamb at school, I'd better explain *why* it was there, and whom I mean when I say *Poetry*, and also when I say *The Sugar Creek Gang*, 'cause maybe you've never heard about us. Then you'll understand that we really weren't trying to get ourselves into trouble when we took that innocent lamb to school that Monday morning.

The idea had first come to us when we were having our gang meeting the second Saturday after school started that fall. We had our meeting in an abandoned graveyard, away up on the other side of Bumblebee Hill, which is a nickname for Strawberry Hill, which we'd given it after we'd killed a bear there, and later fought and licked a tough town gang. In fact the bumblebees helped us lick that tough, swearing bunch of boys.

As I said, the second Saturday after school had started, we had our gang meeting in that spooky old cemetery which they didn't bury people in any more; and that was the time we decided to let Poetry's lamb follow him to school the very next Monday morning.

Right after dinner that Saturday, after I'd wiped the dishes, and Mom and Dad had both said I didn't have to work that afternoon, I made a dive for our kitchen door. I stopped outside only long enough to keep the door from slamming so it wouldn't wake up my little one-year-old baby sister, Charlotte Ann, and then like a wild deer, I gal-

4

loped out across our grassy yard, passed the big walnut tree with the high swing in it, swished across the road and passed our tin mailbox which had on it, *Theodore Collins,* which is my Dad's name; then I touched one hand on the top rail of the rail fence, vaulted over and ran. *Ran,* I tell you, straight down the path through the woods that leads to the spring. At the biggest tree in the woods I swerved to the right and followed another path which had been made by boys' feet, and pretty soon, gasping and panting and swinging my straw hat, I was at the bottom of Bumblebee Hill, where the gang was all supposed to meet first. We all had a spooky feeling about meeting in that graveyard because there were so many stories in the world about graveyards having ghosts in them, so we'd all planned to all go there together, and if there were any ghosts, we could—well, we could all run away together anyway.

I stopped to get rid of some of my extra breath, always having too much after running like that, when just that minute I heard a noise of underbrush crashing and breaking and of a heavy body running. I looked up, and there lumbering toward me was my best friend, Leslie Thompson, whose nickname is *Poetry.* Right that same minute he saw me and began to quote between puffs, one of his more than one hundred memorized poems, and it was about the wind which his heavy breathing had reminded him of. It went something like this:

I saw you toss the kites on high,
And blow the birds about the sky;
And all around I heard you pass
Like ladies' skirts across the grass—
O wind, a-blowing all day long!
O wind, that sings so loud a song!

That was one of my favorite poems, so pretty soon Poetry and I were lying down in the long mashed-down grass, watching the white clouds hanging in the lazy blue sky, and listening to each other catch our breaths; and he started quoting the second verse, getting about halfway through, when he was very suddenly interrupted by somebody's spraying water in his face with a squirt gun.

Even I was half-mad for a jiffy, 'cause some of the water spattered in my face. Besides I was sort of dreaming about the wind which Poetry's poem was describing, and nobody likes to have his thoughts interrupted. Poetry was just saying:

I saw the different things you did
But always, you, yourself, you hid;
I felt you push, I heard you call,
I could not see yourself at all—

Then he started to gasp and sputter, and to get red in his fat face and to roll over and sit up and to say something, when from the bushes behind there came a squawky voice, imitating Poetry's ducklike voice, and it said:

> The rain is raining all around,
> It rains on field and tree;
> It rains on umbrellas here,
> And on the ships at sea.

I knew right away which one of the Sugar Creek Gang it was, 'cause he was the only one of us who was more disgusted than the rest of us with Poetry's poetry, and he was always quoting one of them himself just to make it seem ridiculous. Even if I hadn't heard his voice and seen his pretty brown hair on his hatless head, his pretty blue eyes, and monkey-like face, I'd have known it was Circus, our acrobat; for right that minute, he came cartwheeling toward us in grand style, just like an acrobat on a county fair stage, only actually better.

The next minute Circus and Poetry and I were all in a tangled-up scramble like a bunch of boys in a football game, and Poetry especially was grunting and trying to unroll himself from the rest of us. In fact our six legs and six arms, making twelve altogether, sort of looked like a lot of fishing worms in a knot.

We hadn't any more than unscrambled ourselves when there came more running feet in our direction, and in another minute we were four instead of three. This time it was a spindle-legged little guy with very large, bulging eyes and a different kind of a nose that was crooked at the end. His actual name was Roy Gilbert, but we called him Dragonfly, because his eyes were so enormous—almost bigger than his little head, which a *real* dragonfly's eyes are—only of course, Dragonfly's eyes *aren't*. That little chattering, popeyed member of our gang was always seeing things before the rest of us were, and sometimes he saw things that really weren't there at all. He was right though, when he saw the big savage old bear, which we killed and which I told you about in one of the other Sugar Creek Gang stories, and he was also right the time he saw the bank robber, which we helped capture only the year before. On top of that, Dragonfly was also right when he saw the ghost running, or flying or something, in that same old cemetery one night about a week later.

But that's almost telling you a secret which I've saved until another chapter and which didn't happen until after Poetry's innocent lamb had followed him to school.

Anyway, pretty soon, Big Jim, the leader of our gang, came swishing down the path, and stopped in the shade of the bushes beside us and started catching his breath like the rest of us. I couldn't help but notice that the little fuzzy moustache which he had shaved off just before we had taken our trip to Chicago was still off, with not even a sign of its having begun to grow again. In fact, it hadn't been long enough to shave in the first place. Big Jim was a great leader, I tell you—a fierce fighter, and as strong as anything. His hands were calloused from hard work, which he even *liked* to do.

Each one of us was lying in a different direction, chattering away, and waiting for Little Jim, our smallest, to come. He was nearly always late, because he had to practice his piano lesson right after dinner each Saturday. Say, that little guy was getting to be a grand player, his mom being the best musician in all Sugar Creek territory.

Pretty soon I heard somebody coming. I looked around a corner of the elder bush I was lying under, and sure enough it was Little Jim, just poking along, barefoot, his new, clean blue denim overalls rolled up halfway to his knees and his half-worn-out brown straw hat on backward and his little mouselike face looking very content. He was carrying an ash stick about three feet long, with stripes on it, the stripes having been made with his pocket-knife by cutting off the bark, so that it looked like a great big three-foot-long piece of stick candy.

"Hi, Little Jim!" different ones of us called to him.

9

He kept on doing what he was doing, which was knocking off the tops of different weeds with his stick, not paying any attention to us for a jiffy, then he stooped and rolled up his right overall leg which had just come down. While he was still stooped over, he grunted, "Hi, everybody," and stopped, straightened up, and grinned. Then he flopped himself down beside us just in time to get up with us, for at that same minute from the other direction came little red-haired, freckled-faced Tom Till, the new member of our gang. Little red-haired and fiery-tempered Tom Till was a grand little guy even if his big brother Bob was a prodigal son and had caused us, especially Big Jim, a lot of trouble.

Anyway, the minute Little Jim and Tom got there, the rest of us scrambled to our different-sized bare feet and started up Bumblebee Hill to the cemetery—and you can believe this or not—to run into another mystery, which I'll tell you about as soon as I get to it. Writing a story, you know, is like building a tall building. If you put the top on first, without any good foundation, the house will fall down, so I have to save the top for later—which is the mystery. And the mystery is the ghost which Dragonfly saw one very dark night.

"Here we go," Big Jim called to us, unfolding his long legs and rambling up the hill with the rest of us scrambling after him.

Then Big Jim stopped, looked back at us and with a strange expression on his moustacheless face, said, "Anybody afraid!"

And we yelled a big noisy "No!"—all except Dragonfly, whose mother was what is called a "superstitious" person, and actually believed in such things as ghosts. She even believed that if a black cat ran across the road or street in front of you, it meant you were going to have bad luck. Anyway when Dragonfly didn't act like he was glad we were going up to have our meeting in the old cemetery, I knew the reason why and I felt sorry for him.

"Come on, fraidy-cat!" I said, and grabbed him by the arm, and Poetry grabbed him by the other arm and away we went—as I told you to make some plans that were going to make some of the school children laugh and play and some of them cry and work. We certainly didn't know that when we started up that hill for our first fall gang meeting, that the whole fall was going to be filled with exciting adventures. One especially was going to make my fiery red hair stand on end and scare me and the rest of the gang half to death.

2

IT'S A FUNNY FEELING—walking around in an old graveyard, where some of the gravestones are old and covered with lichen and others have fallen down or maybe been pushed over by ornery boys, and where different kinds of weather have erased the names and whatever else has been chiseled on them.

We pushed our way around through chokecherry shrubs and goldenrod and all kinds of weeds, such as blue vervain, which is a tall, slender weed that grows in nearly every pasture along Sugar Creek. I reached out and pulled off a long, green vervain flower spike, which maybe even a week ago had had a little blue ring of flowers around it, but now didn't have any. Ho-hum, I thought. That means autumn is really almost here, and then'll come winter and we can't go barefoot anymore, or go swimming anymore, or dig our toes into the nice warm sand along Sugar Creek, or lie down in the long brown mashed-down grass—like we would be doing in about a minute.

Poetry, who really is a kind of poetical little guy —big guy, rather—came puffing along beside me, and seeing what I had in my hand, he said, "Our new teacher wants us to gather all kinds of weed seeds this fall, and classify them." He took the long green empty flower spike out of my hand and looked at it like a college professor or something, and said with a deep important-sounding voice, "*That*, Bill Collins, is blue vervain. In the middle of summer, here at the bottom, there was a little purple flower ring, which as summer moved along, slowly crept up the spike, the old flowers dying and the new ones coming out, until finally the ring slipped off the nice green lady's finger—I mean, it slipped off Lucille's finger."

BANG! Something inside me fired up when he said that, and *that* was the end of *that* speech. The next thing he knew, he was lying flat on the grass beside a wild rosebush where I'd shoved him, sticking out my foot to trip him at the same time.

"I don't *like* her!" I yelled down at him, meaning I didn't want anybody to know that I thought Circus' ordinary-looking sister, whose name was Lucille, had nice curls.

You see, ever since last year, when I'd tried to kill a spider for one of Circus' many sisters, some of the gang, Poetry especially, had been teasing me about her. And I wouldn't stand for it. In fact if

14

there's anybody I like less than anybody else, it's some awkward girl, although Circus' sister did have nice curls.

Big Jim took us right out into the middle of the old graveyard to where there was a big pine tree, and right beside it on the west side stood a tall tombstone, with a square base, and the rest of it shaped like a monument in a city park. The grass there was nice and long, so we all dropped down, half-sitting and half-lying, like cows do when they rest and chew their cuds, each one of us chewing grass stems or something, and there we had our meeting.

Pretty soon, while I was lying on my back, with my elbows up and my hands folded under the back of my head, I saw, right up on the tall monument-shaped tombstone, something that made me sit up and gasp. I had the funniest feeling when I realized what I was seeing.

" 'Smatter?" Dragonfly wanted to know, looking scared, and not feeling very good about having the meeting there anyway.

"Look at that, will you?" I sort of half-whispered and pointed toward the name. In fact I was pointing with my finger right toward a carved hand which had one of its fingers pointing up.

Well, we'd all seen that tombstone before, and we'd all read what was on it, but it was something brand-new on it that had made me gasp. That carved hand with one of its fingers pointing up had never been there before.

We sort of stared at it and this is what we saw:

SARAH, BELOVED WIFE
OF
SENETH PADDLER.
Born, Sept. 25, 1865; died Sept. 25, 1902.

Right above the name was the carved hand, pointing straight up toward the top of the tombstone and toward the sky; and at the end of the pointing finger, about an inch above it, was a ribbon-shaped piece of marble, with these words carved on it—with brand-new carving, like it had been done only yesterday:

THERE IS REST IN HEAVEN.

All of us felt very sad for a while because we all knew who Seneth Paddler was, and we knew his wife had been dead for a long time, but none of us had ever thought much about his wife. But that new carving meant that the old man still remembered his wife and was maybe very lonesome for her and wanted to meet her again sometime in heaven.

None of us said anything for a minute, each one of us maybe thinking about what a kind old man

Old Man Paddler was—that grand old long-whiskered man who liked us so well, and whose life we'd all saved once when we'd captured the robber that had him all tied and gagged in his cabin which is up in the hills above the swamp and the old sycamore tree.

Poetry was the first one of us to say anything. I was watching Little Jim's face to see what maybe he was thinking about, and he had a very innocent look like he nearly always does have. He looked away quick when he saw me looking at him and took a swipe at a goldenrod plume with his stick, just as Poetry spoke up and said, "She was only thirty-seven years old," he being especially good in arithmetic.

And Dragonfly said in a voice that sounded like a scared boy's voice coming through a hollow log, "M-my m-mother is just thirty-seven years old."

That started us all to talking in kind of low voices about what happened to people when they died and their bodies were buried somewhere.

"They go straight to heaven, if they're saved," Little Jim said, and of course he was right. He even quoted a Bible verse to prove it, he knowing as many Bible verses as Poetry knew poetry, that being the reason why he was always piping up like that and saying things like that. Little Jim was

17

also the best Christian in the whole gang, and I tell you we were proud of him.

But do you know? When you're in a graveyard and you know there isn't any such thing as a ghost, and when you all of a sudden get to talking about things like that, you feel kind of spooky anyway. Maybe it was what Dragonfly said just then that made *me* feel spooky, I don't know, but right that jiffy he said, "My mother saw an actual honest-to-goodness ghost one time walking right across our front yard at night. It had a crazy voice that sounded like a baby crying and—"

"I don't believe it!" Poetry squawked, interrupting him; and we all agreed with Poetry—all except Dragonfly, of course.

"It could have been one of your dad's white horses," I said, and Circus said with a grin on his monkeylike face, "Or one of your lambs or sheep."

Well, we told a few ghost stories to each other until Dragonfly began to look scared. Then we talked about school, and our new teacher, Miss Lilly, who was very nice and even pretty for a schoolteacher, and she was so kind—so very kind in fact, that it had begun to look like maybe we could whisper in school hours without permission. Every single one of us boys liked her.

Pretty soon we were tired of telling ghost stories, and also tired of trying to convince Dragonfly that

18

his mom had seen only a white horse or a lamb or sheep. The word "lamb" reminded Poetry of a poem which he started to quote in a half-man and half-boy voice, and this is the way the poem went:

> Mary had a little lamb,
>   Its fleece was white as snow,
> And everywhere that Mary went,
>   The lamb was sure to go.
>
> It followed her to school one day,
>   It was against the rule,
> It made the children laugh and play
>   To see a lamb at school.

There were several other verses but the idea was like striking a match to a pile of kerosene-soaked kindling wood. It flared up in our minds and we decided that if Poetry wanted to, he could let his pet lamb follow him to school the very next Monday morning. He would let it follow him to school early, before the teacher came, and would tie it in the woodshed; and then maybe along about ten o'clock, he would ask to be excused, and would go outdoors and untie the lamb and let it see where he went. We all knew of course that it would follow him right into the schoolhouse.

Little Jim didn't exactly like the idea, although there was a mischievous grin on his small face and a twinkle in his very sparkling blue eyes—his eyes were as blue, I thought as I lay there beside him in the tall grass beside Sarah Paddler's tombstone, as blue as the very blue sky up there in the direction toward which the finger was pointing.

Well, we brought it to a vote, and the score was seven to none in favor of Poetry's taking his lamb to school the very next Monday morning—none of us knowing that it was going to be a rainy morning and that there would be a mud puddle for the lamb to fall down in just a few feet from the schoolhouse door, just before Poetry let it follow him inside.

3

AFTER CHURCH the next day, which was Sunday, and after dinner which we always have at noon at our house, Poetry and I went riding on our bicycles and learned something else that was important and had to do with the mystery in the cemetery.

Just for fun while we were riding, we turned into the abandoned lane that leads to the cemetery, getting off and walking and pushing our bikes along with us. After a while we were tired, especially 'cause we were sleepy from having had almost too much dinner. We leaned our bikes against the rail fence and lay down to rest where we talked about different things, especially about our Chicago trip by airplane and also especially about the terrible electric storm which had been below us when we were high up in the sky, and what that storm had done to things around Sugar Creek while we were gone. We also talked about Dragonfly's funny experience when he was up in the plane when he lost his breakfast because he got dizzy.

"He's always a little dizzy," Poetry squawked right beside me, and just that minute Dragonfly himself came running along that abandoned old lane, looking like he was scared half to death and running and panting like a ghost was after him.

"Quick!" he yelled, his voice trembling. "I s-saw it! It's an honest-to-goodness—"

Well, we knew that we were not far from the cemetery, and we guessed that Dragonfly had been down there and had thought he had seen a ghost in the daytime even, so we rolled over in the grass into his way and he stumbled over us, and we had a scramble for a while, but say! Dragonfly wasn't scared at all. He was only excited, and *very* happy.

"It's a cave!" he half screamed. "I s-saw it myself with my own eyes!" which of course, I thought, didn't make it so.

He unscrambled himself from us, jumped to his feet and started to run, yelling back at us, "Hurry up! Follow me and I'll show you."

Say, that little spindle-legged guy was so excited, that we came to quick life, left our bikes where they were leaning up against the fence, and streaked down the lane after Dragonfly.

Lickety-sizzle, leap, dodge, whoopee, zip-zip-zip, swish—we followed Dragonfly's flying feet, past the tumbledown old cemetery, over another rail fence and went sailing down Bumblebee Hill where we'd

22

killed the fierce mother bear the year before and on toward the spring and to the sycamore tree which grew on the side of the hill right above Sugar Creek itself. There Dragonfly stopped and yelled, "Look! See it!"

We looked and panted for breath and couldn't believe it, and yet we had to, 'cause right there it was, a great big hole in the side of the hill, at the base of the sycamore tree. Say! That old sycamore tree had been struck by lightning and there was a great big long fierce-looking gash running right down the trunk to the roots and also into the ground. And right there before our eyes we saw that the lightning had opened up for us an honest-to-goodness cave. As far back inside as we could see it was still cave, and very dark and black, although the entrance was small, just about the size of a boy like Poetry, which of course *wasn't* small.

Just that minute we saw somebody's red head push its way out, and it was Little Tom Till himself; then out came Circus' curly brown head and his monkey face; then Big Jim's brown hair and his square jaws, followed by Little Jim's blue eyes and mouselike face and mischievous grin—and we were all there.

We found out afterward that Dragonfly had actually found the cave himself, when he and the rest of the gang had been walking around that afternoon, and they had sent him to hunt up Poetry and me.

Of course Poetry and I wanted to go inside, which we did, and pretty soon all of us were in. It really wasn't much of a cave, only about ten feet across each way and only about seven feet high, but it had a rock wall all around and a rock roof, so we knew it would be a safe place for us to play and wouldn't cave in on us, like a dirt roof or a sand roof might, and our parents wouldn't worry about us when we played there. We all knew it wasn't safe to play in a cave with a dirt or a sand roof, 'cause sometimes they caved in and buried boys alive, smothering them to death.

Say, Big Jim had already been home for some candles. He set two of them, one on each side up on a little ledge of rock, and lit them. We looked funny to each other, sitting there in a sort of half-circle with the candles flickering and our faces covered with moving shadows. We sat around telling stories and imagining we were pirates or somebody, when all of a sudden, Poetry squawked, "Listen! I hear something!"

We all stopped chattering and listened and we *did* hear something, we thought, and then we *didn't* think it, 'cause everything was quiet.

Then Big Jim whispered in a ghostlike voice, and with a hideous grin on his face, "It might be a *ghost!''* His voice was half-whisper and half-growl. Dragonfly who was sitting with his back propped up against my shoulder, jumped like he had heard a shot, 'cause he was the only one of us who believed in ghosts.

Well, it was too nice an afternoon to stay in a dark cave, so we decided to go outside a while and do something else, when Poetry caught at my shirt and whispered, "Wait a minute!"

I waited a minute and he pulled me back inside a little farther and said, "Sh! Listen right here against this side!"

I laid my head against a slab of rock which was against the wall and it was as plain as day, the thing I heard. It sounded kind of spooky at first, and of course there just wasn't any sense to it, but it sounded like somebody pounding with something very far away.

We sat up then and looked at each other's faces in the candlelight—his big fat face and my freckled one—and we knew we had actually discovered something. There was a noise like somebody pounding, and not with a hammer either, but like somebody with a pickax trying to dig his way out of somewhere.

Or else it sounded like something else. As you maybe know Poetry was always imagining himself to be a detective, so he whispered to me and said,

"This is a secret, Bill Collins. Promise me you won't tell a soul."

We shook hands in what we called a solemn pledge not to tell anybody what we'd heard.

Then I moved my freckled face over to one of the candles and Poetry moved his fat face toward the other one, and *puff,* out went the two candles in two breaths. In another minute we were outside in the very bright sunlight which was playing and dancing everywhere and making the little wavelets on Sugar Creek sparkle like they were happy, which maybe they were.

I hadn't been out of the cave more than a jiffy when I saw Little Jim standing up there by the syc-amore tree with his ash stick striking away at some of the loose bark and knocking it off just for fun. I looked at Poetry and he looked at me, and we sighed at each other.

"You and your swell detective ideas!" I said to him.

"*My* idea!" he said disgustedly. "Who *said* it was my idea?"

With that, Poetry grinned at me like he had known all the time it was Little Jim with his stick and had been fooling me. Just the same, he put his fat forefinger up to his pursed lips and quoted from one of his one hundred and one poems:

Two ears and only one mouth have you,
    The reason I think is clear:
It teaches, my child, that it will not do
    To talk about all you hear.

Well, we all did different things, having lots of fun, and pretty soon, it got to be late in the afternoon. Poetry and I and the rest of the gang couldn't think of anything we all wanted to do together, so after we had had a meeting there by the sycamore tree and agreed to meet at the cave next time, in fact to all bring a blanket from home if our parents would let us, and all sleep there some night— maybe the very next Friday night, if our parents would let us—we adjourned and each one went whichever way he wanted to with whomever he wanted to to our different homes. Poetry and I went together 'cause our bikes were up there beyond Bumblebee Hill waiting for us. Neither one of us knew we were going to run right smack into another interesting experience before we got home.

4

WELL, POETRY AND I rambled back toward Bumble-bee Hill, puffed our way up to the top, climbed over the old vine-covered rail fence, pushed our way around through the chokecherry shrubs, picking and eating some of the darkish purple, winy-flavored, shiny-skinned cherries and getting our lips stained at the same time.

Pretty soon we came to Sarah Paddler's grave, when all of a sudden Poetry gasped and said, "Come here a minute, will you!"

I poked along over to where he was standing and reading something on a very old tombstone, and would you believe it? It said on that stone, which was tall and flat and had a carved picture of the Good Shepherd at the top, leaning out over the edge of a mountain to save a little lonely lamb from falling:

DANIEL, JOHN AND WILLIAM,
Three sons of
Seneth and Sarah Paddler,
Died Dec. 6, 1895.

There was more on the stone which the weather had rubbed out, but I remembered that my Dad had once told me that Old Man Paddler had had three sons a very long time ago, and that they had all died, and that was the reason he liked boys so well, and maybe was why he was so extra kind to the Sugar Creek Gang.

We stood there looking at the names and feeling and thinking different things, when Poetry said, "I wonder what they died of?"

"I don't know," I said. "Smallpox maybe," which is a very dangerous contagious disease against which every boy and even every girl ought to be vaccinated, so they won't get it. Doctors will even do it free for poor people.

I was looking at the name "William" and wondering how old he had been. You know my name is "William," that is, my first name is. Just that minute we heard somebody coming, so we beat it down the fence, climbed over and flopped down in the grass of the abandoned lane not far from our bicycles and watched. In a jiffy we saw an old man hobbling along—an old man with long white whiskers and very white hair. He was carrying a yardstick in one hand and a sickle and a potted plant of some kind in the other.

"*Shhh!*" Poetry shushed me when I started to whisper something. So I shushed and we both watched, though we knew right away it was Old Man Paddler himself who had paid for our airplane trip to Chicago which we'd had week before last, and who had also paid for our camping trip up north which you already know about.

I was looking through the bottom rails of the fence and through the flannellike leaves of a big mullein stalk, of which there were maybe a dozen all around us. In fact I had a mullein leaf in my hand right that minute and I thought how nice and soft it was, and how white the soft hairs on its very green leaves were, and of course I was wondering what that old man was doing out there. But say, he knew what he was doing all right. He very carefully cut the grass and weeds away from the base of the tombstones—from his wife's and from the one that had his boys' names on it—and then he set the potted plant down at his wife's grave. The next thing we knew he was standing there with his black hat hanging on a bush and he was looking up toward the sky which had white clouds in it as white as his hair, and he began to talk out loud to Someone in a trembling old voice, and this is a part of what he said: "Dear Father in heaven . . . and in my heart I'm getting lonesome for my boys and my Sarah, and I'm getting very old."

Just then a little whirlwind which had been coming across the graveyard, rattled and twisted the bushes and blew the old man's hair across his fore-head, and also blew away the sound of his words. He was through praying anyway, I guess, for he put his hat back on his head and started doing the strangest thing I ever heard of.

Poetry reached out his fat hand and touched mine to be sure I was watching, and I was, and that old man stood his yardstick up against Sarah Paddler's tombstone and began to measure how tall it was. He did the same to the width, at the bottom and at the top and in the middle. He wrote down the measurements in a little notebook like the one I used at school, then he looked around in different directions, took his yardstick and sickle and moved away, winding around among the weeds and through the vervain, some of which still had little blue flower rings around them, at the top especially, through the chokecherries to the fence and climbed through—that is, almost. He got his white shirt caught on a barbed wire, and there he was, stuck. He couldn't go backward or forward, or sidewise either, unless he wanted to tear his shirt still worse.

Well, my parents had taught me to be especially kind to all old people, never to make fun of them and to be very courteous and helpful, so before I knew it, I'd called, "Wait a minute, Mr. Paddler, I'll help you!"

The next thing I knew, I was on my bare feet, running toward him. Poetry got there as quick as I did. In a flash we had his shirt loose, and the old man crawled through.

Say, he certainly was grateful. After he had thanked us, he started to go on toward his home which I knew was up in the hills in an old cabin that looked like the one Abraham Lincoln was born in, with a clapboard roof and different things that made it look like what my mom called "romantic."

I noticed just that minute that he had torn a jagged hole about three inches in different directions in his shirt, and I also noticed that his old hands were kind of gnarled like the twisted grain in a block of wood, and I knew it would be hard for him to handle a small needle, so I said, "Mr. Paddler, if you'll come over to our·house tomorrow, my mom will be glad to sew up that rip in your shirt."

He turned around and tried to stretch his neck around far enough to see his back and couldn't, so he smiled—sure he did! I couldn't see it because of his long beard, but I saw the twinkles in his kind old eyes and I knew that a man couldn't have twinkles like that in his eyes and keep a straight face.

"Thank you, Bill," he said; then all of a sudden he frowned, and all the twinkles left his eyes as he said in his trembling old voice, "I used to have a boy of my own named Bill. He was just about your age." His voice stopped, and he swallowed a lump or something in his throat, then he turned and shuffled away, and we went on toward home ourselves, getting our bikes first. Tomorrow, we told each other, we would be having a lot of fun. Tomorrow, Poetry's innocent lamb whose fleece was as white as snow, would follow him to our red schoolhouse, and all the children would laugh and play to see a lamb at school—'cause it was, of course, against the rule.

"So long," Poetry puffed at my gate when I turned in and came riding into our barnyard where Dad was just going out to the barn with two great big milk pails, with our old black and white mixy cat—her name was *Mixy*, you know—following along behind him and mewing like everything, already hungry for her supper.

"Hurry up, Bill!" Dad called cheerfully. My wristwatch told me I was later than I should have been 'cause we always had to do our chores early on Sundays because all of us went to church every Sunday night, which nearly all the Sugar Creek Gang's parents did except Dragonfly's, which is why that little balloon-eyed member of our gang didn't know much about the Bible, only what he got from us, and especially from Little Jim.

Just that second I heard somebody whistle up the road, and I looked and it was Poetry, waving a final good-bye, meaning, "Don't forget tomorrow!"

Which I never did—and never will as long as I live.

5

In the middle of that night, I woke up, with lightning playing around in the sky and thunder growling in the distance, and that's how there happened to be mud puddles in the lane the next day, when I stopped at Poetry's house to get him on my way to school. Generally I didn't stop for him because I had to go early, to get there before the teacher and open the windows, and maybe do a little dusting. Every evening after school it was my job to sweep the schoolhouse floor, and lock up after the teacher had gone, unless for some reason she stayed longer than I did.

Well, in a jiffy when I got to Poetry's house, there he came, carrying his red dinner pail, and right behind him crowding close and following all around him was his innocent lamb, with a rope around its neck, so it wouldn't get away from him after he'd fed it, which it sometimes would if he didn't watch out.

As you know our plan was to tie the lamb in the woodshed, and lock the door. It happened there was only one key to that door and we kept it in a special place which nobody knew about except the teacher and me and—well, I had to tell Poetry, so later on, after school should have started, and he went outdoors, he could get the key, unlock the door, and the lamb would do the rest.

I had on my rubbers, because the mud and water were everywhere, and so did Poetry, but the lamb's mother hadn't taught him anything like that so by the time we got to school the lamb was plenty muddy around the feet and legs. When I saw the great big brown mud puddle not far from our schoolhouse door, which the township trustee, who was Little Jim's dad, would have to have filled with gravel soon, I said to Poetry, "See to it that he doesn't get all splashed up in the puddle, or you'll have to mop the floor."

Poetry grinned and said, standing beside the little soft-eyed woolly lamb and with his own eyes looking just as innocent, "Lambs don't walk in puddles if they can help it. That's why their mothers never make them wear rubbers."

"Just the same," I said, "I think we ought to make him wipe his feet on the mat here."

Right away I opened the door after unlocking it and picked up the nice brown mat and set it just outside the door for the lamb to wipe its feet on.

Say, that lamb acted like he was just waiting to jump up there on that step, for the second Poetry stepped up, the lamb was right at his heels, walking

around in every direction at once all over the little
six-by-eight porch, and getting lamb tracks on it.

"Hey!" I yelled to Poetry. "Get him out of here!"
which Poetry did, getting *himself* out of there first.
As it was I would have to get the mop and wipe all
the mud off.

Well, we went to the woodshed, locked the lamb
inside, and I decided to keep the key in my pocket,
so in case some of the other members of the gang
came early to school, they wouldn't find the key
and go in and look at the lamb and maybe accidentally let it get out.

As soon as the battered old woodshed door was
locked, Poetry and I walked back toward the schoolhouse door, stopping on the way at the tall, long-
handled iron pump to get a drink out of the drinking cups we had in our dinner pails.

Poetry and I took off our rubbers and went inside the schoolhouse, where I opened the windows
to let fresh air go through, and Poetry went to the
blackboard and started working on an arithmetic
problem which he had been having trouble with
the week before. Pretty soon, after I had dusted
the teacher's desk and the top of the globe of the
world, and was getting ready to sweep up some
dust over in a corner where I'd missed it the last
time I'd swept the floor, there was a shadow in the
open doorway. I looked up quick and there was

popeyed Dragonfly walking right in without taking off his rubbers. In fact, he didn't have any on.

"HEY!" I yelled indignantly at him, with my eyebrows down like my Dad's are when he is angry at something or somebody or me, and Dragonfly stopped stock-still.

" 'Smatter?" he called. "Where's the lamb?"

"Listen, you!" I exclaimed to him, waving my broom at him and starting toward him on the half-run, "You get yourself out of here and wipe your feet on the mat—or out on the grass *first*, and then the mat, and keep *still* about the lamb!"

Dragonfly obeyed as meekly as an innocent lamb is supposed to, then he came back in, and walked around between the rows of seats, and around the big Poetry-shaped iron stove in the middle of the room. Finally he stopped in front of our seven-inch-thick dictionary which always lies down open or shut on a low shelf on the south wall near a window. He started looking up different words while Poetry kept working away with noisy chalk on the blackboard and I kept on sweeping a little, dusting and acting important, and feeling the same way, when all of a sudden Dragonfly said, "My mom saw another ghost last night!"

I stopped stock-still, stopped sweeping and said saucily, "Stop saying stuff like that! You know there isn't any such thing as a ghost."

40

And Dragonfly replied equally as saucily as I had, "*You* know it and *I* know it, but my *mother* doesn't know it. Say, come here, will you?" Dragonfly raised his voice excitedly, and in a jiffy Poetry and I were there, Poetry dropping an eraser and a piece of chalk on the way, and I stopping to pick up the broom I'd just dropped.

"See here!" Dragonfly said. "Here's what it says a ghost is!"

I looked at the place where his crooked fingernail was pointing and it said: "Ghost, *noun*, 1. A disembodied spirit."

"What's *disembodied* mean?" Dragonfly wanted to know, and for a second I knew he was believing the same thing his mother believed.

I sighed and looked at Poetry who, like he had done yesterday, put his fat forefinger up to his pursed lips and said, "Two ears and only one mouth have you."

Poetry interrupted himself then and said, "Here, let's look up the word *disembodied*," which he did, and pretty soon my blue-gray eyes and Poetry's sky-blue ones and Dragonfly's brown balloon-shaped ones were all looking at the definition of the word *disembody* and Poetry's squawky voice was reading it, and it was: "*verb*, *transitive*, to free from the body." And that meant a ghost was a spirit free from its body.

41

"See there!" Dragonfly said triumphantly. "It doesn't say there *isn't* any such thing!" which it didn't, and I was remembering the pounding noise I'd heard in the cave yesterday, which might have been Little Jim's stick against the old sycamore tree, and probably was.

Well, pretty soon Miss Lilly would be there, and a little later the rest of the seventeen pupils, which was all the children that came to our grand little red brick schoolhouse. Even though it had rained hard during the night, the sun was out now and it was going to be a very cheerful day, and hard for us to keep the grins off when we thought of the lamb that was locked up out in the woodshed, and would stay there until Poetry went out to let it out.

Pretty soon we heard a car and it was Miss Lilly herself, in her green coupé, stopping right under the big sugar tree not far from the tall, long-handled pump. Say, Miss Lilly sort of looked like a lily that morning, I thought, as she stepped out onto the grass-covered ground, with her pretty long brown hair very carefully combed like Little Jim's pretty mom combs hers. She was wearing a brown and white dress, the white being actual lilies—that is, lily designs or something, and she had several books and a lunch basket, which as quick as we could get to her car Poetry and Dragonfly and I offered to carry into the schoolhouse.

"Good morning, boys!" her musical voice said to us very cheerfully, and she smiled at us in a way that made me desire to study hard all day—that is, as soon as I could after the lamb had come in.

Just that minute we heard a sound coming from the woodshed like something was trying to get out the door, and we also heard a lamb bleating.

I could feel my hair acting funny under my cap, and I could see Poetry's face turn red and Dragonfly's eyes get bigger.

Miss Lilly looked around quick and exclaimed, "What *was* that?"

And Poetry squawked indifferently, looking at me before I could look away, "*That*—that was probably a—maybe some new kind of bird singing. There's always some new bird around."

At that Miss Lilly laughed and said, "You always have an answer, don't you! It is a nice day, isn't it?" Then she started toward the door of the school, with us carrying the different things for her.

Whew! I thought. *That* was a close shave! She had actually heard the lamb and she could have also seen the little cloven-foot tracks there in the mud too, if she had looked, but she hadn't.

Well, right after that children started to come from different directions, some across the fields, some down the lane and others on the road. Pretty soon our gang was all there, which is all the boys there were in our school, the rest of the children being just girls, some big and some little and most of them with different colored and different sized hair ribbons in their different colored hair, and all of them carrying dinner pails and some of them books. They all come through the little wooden gate not far from the tall, long-handled iron pump, playing and saying different things to each other, most of them being noisy, except a few very bashful girls who were coming to school for the very first time that year.

Big Jim was standing right beside me when Sylvia's little sister came walking through the gate. Sylvia, you know, is our minister's oldest daughter, and she had been in the eighth grade the year before and was going to town to high school this year. Big Jim had had to stay out of school one whole year before he had moved into Sugar Creek territory a few years ago, because he had had an operation. So he was still in grade school, for which we were very glad.

All of a sudden, Sylvia's little sister, Jeanelle, came sidling over to Big Jim with her pigtails flopping down on her neck and she handed him something which I guessed was a note. Big Jim shoved it into his pocket quick, started whistling and walking off across the schoolyard by himself, yawning

and acting indifferent and stretching his arms lazi-
ly.

Pretty soon the last bell rang, and all of us that
were outside went storming in—that is, we went
like lions up to as far as the door, then we went
inside like a lot of lambs. Just as we got to the
door, I slipped the woodshed key to Poetry, who
shoved it into one of his pockets and went innocent-
ly to his seat across the room from me.

In a jiffy we were quiet, with the smallest kids
sitting in the front seats near the teacher's desk.
First thing on the program was opening exercises,
which lasted for ten minutes and was the reading of
an interesting Bible story out of a children's Bible
storybook, and then a short prayer by Miss Lilly
herself, with all of us bowing our heads reverently.
Then we started off the day's work studying and re-
citing and keeping quiet, which is harder even than
hard work unless you are *interested* in your work.

First, the first grade did some slow, monotonous
reading, which made it hard for me to study, 'cause
in a one-room schoolhouse you have to study most
of the time while somebody else is talking. It was
especially hard for me, for just that minute I was
looking at an arithmetic problem which said, "Mr.
Brown had thirty-seven sheep whose wool averaged
seven pounds each. He sold the wool at one dollar
per pound, and deposited one half of the money in

45

the State Bank, one third of it in the Security Bank and paid his lumber bill with the remaining sum. How much was his lumber bill?"

I looked out of the corner of my eye at Poetry who was looking at me out of the corner of his eye, and he snickered, 'cause he was trying to work the same arithmetic problem I was.

When Miss Lilly turned around at the blackboard, our faces were as blank as the sheet of paper I was supposed to be working problems on, as also was Poetry's.

Well, we suffered along for ten or fifteen minutes, each one of the Sugar Creek Gang, even Little Jim, acting very busy, until all of a sudden Poetry raised one of his fat hands and asked to be excused. Miss Lilly looked at him in a blank way like teachers do when they are thinking about something else, nodded her brown head absentmindedly, and Poetry turned sideways, set his feet in the aisle, stood up and started walking heavily because his feet are big and he is very heavy himself, toward the only door the schoolhouse had. He pushed open the screen and went out. I kept my face straight with my eyes on my arithmetic, trying to figure out how much Mr. Brown owed the lumberyard and how many pounds of wool his thirty-seven sheep had. I frowned and scowled at that problem and at the thousand or more snickers which were trying to burst out of my mouth every second.

Some of the windows of the school were still open. I heard Poetry walking toward the woodshed, then I heard the rattle of a steel lock and I even thought I heard the sound of the key turning in the lock, then I heard the door swing open, *squeak-squeak-squeak*. Why on earth, I thought, didn't we think to oil that woodshed door before we did anything else? And then, a little later, I heard a lot of steps coming toward the school on the gravel just outside the door.

I was right close to the window, so I took a quick sideways glance, and say! Poetry looked worried. He had lost his nerve or something and was trying to get the lamb to change its mind about following him inside, I supposed. Anyway, it was all around him and in front of him and behind him at the same time, and then—well, I heard some water splashing and I knew what *that* meant—with a mud puddle not far from the schoolhouse door. Right away I heard steps on the roofless porch, the door opening, and a scuffling noise; and the next thing I knew there was Poetry coming in and trying to keep the lamb out—or pretending to, I couldn't tell which—and then the lamb was inside. Inside! A lamb in our schoolhouse! A *muddy* lamb, with *very* muddy feet!

6

Mary had a little lamb,
    Its fleece was white as snow,
And everywhere that Mary went,
    The lamb was sure to go.

It followed her to school one day—
    It was against the rule;
It made the children laugh and play
    To see a lamb at school.

And so the teacher put him out.

THAT'S THE WAY the poem goes, and it certainly sounds like an innocent little jingle, but when you try to act it out in real life like we did—well, it certainly wasn't.

Somebody ought to rewrite that poem and make it something like this:

Poetry had a little lamb,
    Its fleece a dirty black;
The only place its wool was white
    Was high upon its back.

It followed him to school one day,
   It made the teacher sick,
I couldn't study geography,
   Nor get my 'rithmetic.

The children didn't laugh or play,
   It made them stare and blush,
And over all that one-room school,
   There came an awful hush.

And Big Jim, Little Jim and Tom,
   And Circus, too, and me
And Dragonfly—the six of us,
   Were scared as Poetry.

Something like that would make a good start for a new poem which would be more true to life than the one about Mary's innocent lamb. Say, there wasn't anything very innocent about our lamb that day. The very minute it and Poetry got inside, it began to act like it was wild. It started running around in different directions, scared and bleating, making muddy tracks everywhere, and making the little girls cry. It upset a mop pail which was by the door under the long shelf where the dinner pails were all in a row, and that mop pail went banging and rolling and emptying its soapy water in different directions all over the floor.

And that's how I happened to have to stay in at recess to mop up the whole mess. In fact, we had recess right away, a nice long one for everybody except some of us.

Quick as a flash when that pail of soapy water was turned over and different ones of us raised up our feet quick when it went in our direction, like a farmer getting his chickens and hogs out of the way when Sugar Creek goes on a rampage in the spring, Miss Lilly called us to order, saying, "All right, everybody! Quiet, please!"

She stood there behind her desk like a queen, her face saying there was going to be some kind of trouble but not saying what.

Well, as soon as we all quieted down, the lamb did the same thing. Then Miss Lilly said to Poetry very sternly, "Leslie, will you please open the door and lead the animal out!"

Leslie Poetry Thompson was as meek as a lamb was supposed to be. He stood to his big feet and said politely, "Yes, ma'am!" He walked heavily to the door and opened it, the lamb all of a sudden seeing him and getting there almost as quick as he did, and getting out even quicker, making a noise as it scampered across the roofless porch and out onto the graveled walk; and I, looking around quick, saw it stop and lift its head and look back up to the door at Poetry.

After that, Miss Lilly said to all the rest of us,

"There will be a short recess for everyone except the boys. Go quietly, please. Turn."

The girls turned, set their feet out in the aisles, each one trying to miss the soapy water; then Miss Lilly said, "Stand," and they stood, and waited for her to say, "Pass," which she did, and they passed out very quietly, walking like they were walking on eggs which might break any minute.

The second the last girl was out, Miss Lilly went to the door and shut it and walked back to the front of the room and stood there beside her desk with one hand resting on the top of the globe. Her face was sober and it looked as if the whole world was going to be against us. We didn't know what to expect and my heart was pounding. Little Jim who was sitting across the aisle from me was even white, he was so tense inside. Poetry for once in his life didn't look mischievous, and Circus didn't have any tree he could climb to let off some of the extra steam that was almost all the time inside him trying to get out. Dragonfly looked like he was seeing one of his mother's ghosts. Big Jim looked very calm, and he had one of his hands in one of his pockets where probably the note was which Sylvia's little sister had given him, I thought. Little Tom Till's freckled face and red hair looked like they always do—his face a little dirty, his hair a little mussed up in different places, especially at the top of the back where he had what is called a "cow-lick," which means a place where the hair starts growing in different directions. It acutally does look like a place on a calf's back where our old Brindle cow has just licked it with her rough tongue, or else it looks like a place on the long-napped reddish-brown rug in our front room after a boy has scraped his foot over it.

Miss Lilly stood there for a long time with her hands on the world. I could tell she was thinking what to do with us, and couldn't decide. There was a very pretty sparkling ring on her hand, which looked like a diamond, and I noticed that Big Jim was looking at it and admiring it, and maybe wasn't thinking about any muddy lamb.

Then Miss Lilly cleared her voice which didn't need clearing and said to Poetry, "Leslie, will you step outside please and bring your lamb in again?"

He stared at her like he couldn't believe it, until she said firmly, *"Now, please!"*

Poetry walked to the door, looked out, and called the lamb by name, which was "Jerry," and the lamb, seeing him, was on the steps right away. Pretty soon Poetry and the lamb were inside again.

Say, that lamb, even though it was still dirty, was as meek as could be. It even let Miss Lilly put her hand on it, which she did, stroking it, letting her hand move from its forehead across its poll, which

53

is its head, and down its neck to its withers, which is the part of the lamb where its neck and back meet.

Of course Poetry had to stand beside her and the lamb, to make it stay there, but it acted like it liked to have her stroke it—just like a kitten acts, purring to show you it *really* does.

Well, I knew by the expression that came into Miss Lilly's soft blue eyes that she wasn't going to scold us. Instead, her voice got a faraway expression in it, just like her eyes had and she said, "Boys, members of the Sugar Creek Gang, I wonder if you remember the story of a man named John who lived a long time ago in a beautiful little country, right in the very center of the world, known now as Palestine. He was standing one day, speaking to a very large crowd of people who had come out along a river to listen to him. This man John was a prophet of the God who made the whole world. He had just finished preaching a sermon and all of a sudden, there came Someone walking along the river, a strong young Man whose life was clean and pure, and who had never done a wrong thing in His life.

"That young Man, strong and pure in mind and body, walked toward John before all the people; and seeing Him, John raised his great voice and cried out to the people, 'Behold the Lamb of God that taketh away the sin of the world!' " Miss Lilly raised her voice to say that.

And then she lowered her voice, stopped speaking in fact, and her face still had that very quiet, faraway look in it as she said, stroking the little lamb's head and neck, "That young Man was the only Man in all the history of the world who could have taken away—taken away—"

Then Miss Lilly's faraway voice stopped speaking again; and there were tears in her eyes, when she decided to go on. First she looked at each one of us like she wasn't seeing us, and then she very gently stroked the head and forehead of the lamb with one hand, looking at it quietly. Then she turned her pretty face and looked across to the globe of the world where her other hand was resting and said, "This young Man's name was—the Lord Jesus Christ. He is the one of whom John the Baptist said, 'Behold the Lamb of God that taketh away the sin of the world.' "

I looked across a few aisles to where Little Jim was sitting with his little hands in front of him on the top of his desk. His eyes were glued to Miss Lilly, with his fists all doubled up and I thought I saw him swallow something in his throat. Circus was sitting with his hands on his knees under the desk. Tom Till had his feet out in the aisle, but was leaning forward sideways with his chin resting on the back of his hands with his elbows on the desk. Poetry was moving one of his hands around in his desk, feeling for something, which in a jiffy he found and it was his New Testament, which he started to open right away and look up the story Miss Lilly had just told us.

Big Jim and I weren't doing anything except listening, but something very strange was going on in my mind. All the time while she was talking so kindly, I kept thinking of the One she was talking about, and I kept looking at the big round world with millions of people on it, who didn't even know yet that Somebody had died for their sins, and I wished everybody who knew about it would hurry up and tell everybody else. I even wished I would tell a lot of people myself. I forgot all about the mischievous prank the Sugar Creek Gang had just played.

Right that minute while those different thoughts were splashing around in my mind, Miss Lilly said, raising her voice, "And now, Leslie, if you will put your lamb out to pasture, and if you, Bill, will get busy with the mop and pail we'll have the schoolhouse ready for business in a few minutes."

What? I thought. *No punishment! No scolding!*

But there wasn't, not even a frown. And do you know what? Just that quick, I decided I liked our teacher very much, and someday when I got big enough to, I was going to be a very special friend of somebody just like her, and protect her from all kinds of danger, such as wolves howling at night, or some gangster, or save her from drowning or something. And if she was afraid of a spider or a mouse like most girls and even women are, I'd kill one of them for her too.

Well, all the Sugar Creek Gang went to work on that schoolhouse floor, and in almost less than no time, it was ready for occupation. The bell rang and the girls came back in, all them looking at us to see if any of us had had a licking, and probably wishing we had, like girls sometimes do, and none of us had.

School started again and went on as usual, with nothing important happening until noon that day, when the gang was lying out in the shade of a big ash tree at the west end of our big schoolyard, and Big Jim pulled a folded piece of paper out of his pocket and read it to us—the same note Sylvia's little sister had given him in the morning. Say! What that note said was plenty!

Plenty!

7

WE WERE ALL LYING DOWN under the big ash tree,
with our heads together and our bodies resting
seven different directions like a big human wheel
with seven spokes, with the lower end of each spoke
dividing like the fork of a boy's slingshot, only
there wasn't any rim on the wheel and some of the
spokes were shorter than some of the others.

Big Jim took the note out of his pocket and asked
us to get ready to listen to something important.
Say, it wasn't from Sylvia at all, but was printed
in somebody's awkward style, maybe a boy's, and
whoever had done it had probably used an indelible pencil, wetting the pencil with a sponge or
something, or if he was an ignorant boy he might
have done it with his tongue or lips. Indelible pencil is poison, you know, if you wet it that way.

Well, I was watching the almost imaginary fuzz
on Big Jim's upper lip while he was talking and
getting ready to read.

This is what the note said:

> Just to warn you that the cave at the base
> of the old sycamore tree is haunted. So please
> STAY AWAY!

I don't know what made me do it, but all of a sudden I lifted my eyes and looked at Dragonfly, and he was acting a little funny, I thought. His eyes were big like they always are and he looked very innocent. But just that second I looked under his crooked nose which turns south at the end, and I saw with my own eyes a little bit of purple marking on his big teeth which were too big for his small face and would be until his face grew some more.

I looked from Dragonfly's funny face to Poetry's fat one, and Poetry was already looking at my freckled one. He winked at me and I remembered the pounding noise he and I had heard the day before in the cave, and the water running that sounded like a small underground spring. I also remembered his poem about not talking about all you see and hear.

There wasn't any name signed to the note, I noticed, and so did all of us, as right that minute our nice wagon wheel with its seven divided spokes was getting all broken up, and all of us were sitting in an interested huddle around Big Jim. Such crazy printing I had never seen, and the note was so short that it almost made me feel creepy. *What if the cave* was *haunted?* I thought. What if Dragonfly's mother had been right?

And then I felt Little Jim's hand, which was lying on my shoulder, catch hold of my suspender like he was glad to have something to hold onto, and I knew that even though he *knew* there wasn't any such thing as a ghost, he still wondered if there might not be maybe just *one!*

Just that minute also, I clapped my hand over my mouth to stop myself from asking Big Jim, "How come Sylvia's little sister Jeanelle gave the note to you?" I would ask that later, I thought.

We lay there talking and still talking, saying there isn't any such thing as a ghost and Dragonfly saying there *might* be. Every now and then I saw the purple on his two big central incisors, which is the name of the two biggest front teeth a boy has; but I decided to keep still for a while, and talk it over with Poetry later.

We also talked a little about the lamb at school and we also watched the girls on the other side of the schoolyard, who were walking around with their arms linked or with their arms around each other the way some girls sometimes do. Circus did a few acrobatic stunts on a strong limb of the ash tree, which hung down real low to the ground, and pretty soon Big Jim said, "Let's have a meeting," which we did. We gathered around him in a tangled-up circle, some of us on our elbows, and some of us on our knees and on each other's elbows and knees, and Big Jim said, "Will someone make a motion to the effect that we have a meeting at the cave next Friday night—that is, that we take our blankets and sleep in the cave just to show the ghosts that there aren't any?"

We looked at each other, and most of us looked at Dragonfly and I said to that popeyed person, nodding my red head to him at the same time, "Go ahead and make the motion."

"I *will* not," he said, and I saw the purple stains on his incisors again.

"You're a scaredy-cat," Poetry said to him, and Big Jim's voice said gruffly, "Order, please!" and there was.

Just then Circus said, "I move we sleep in the cave next Friday night."

"Second the motion," I said.

"Third it," Poetry squawked, and Big Jim said, "Order" again.

Then he said, "It has been moved and seconded that we, all of us including Dragonfly, sleep in the cave next Friday night. Are you ready for the question?"

We were, so he said, "All in favor, please respond by the uplifted hand."

Dragonfly cut in then, and said, "You forgot to ask if there were any remarks."

Big Jim frowned and said, "Well, are there any?

Anybody afraid to sleep in a cave—an innocent cave?" And nobody was.

The motion was carried, which means that most of us voted "Yes." We sat and lay and sprawled there on the long grass, each one of us except Dragonfly having his hand up, although I couldn't help but notice that Little Jim's hand wasn't very high and the fingers were all pressed tight together and his hand was very close to his face, right beside his right blue eye which had a hollow look in it. Tom Till waited till the rest of us had voted "Yes" before he did the same thing.

Pretty soon we heard the schoolbell ring for the last time, the five-minute bell having rung a few jiffies before, in fact it seemed like only a minute before. Then we all, the whole school of seventeen, started running lickety-sizzle toward that one-room schoolhouse's only door, which was painted a kind of bluish-gray and had a white knob, which had to be washed often to *keep* it white. I couldn't help but remember the time I had been up north on our camping trip fishing for bluegills with a worm and had looked down into the water under the boat. Say! The minute the worm went down-down-down about seventeen different sizes and kinds of fish had darted toward it—the worm *and* the hook— perch, bluegills, rock bass and others.

Poetry and I stayed behind a little and on the way I said, "Did you notice Dragonfly's teeth?"

"Sure," he said, "big enough to eat up Little Red Riding Hood's grandmother."

"I mean," I explained, "did you notice their color? There were indelible pencil stains on them."

"*What!*" he said, and stopped stock-still.

"Actually," I said.

Just that minute his lamb, which had been peacefully under the big maple tree near the big tall long-handled iron pump, raised its innocent head and started toward us on a half-run, with its tail flapping along behind it. That reminded Poetry of a poem which right away he started to quote, which made us both a little late for school. The poem was:

> Little Bo-Peep has lost her sheep,
> And can't tell where to find them;
> Leave them alone and they'll come home
> Bringing their tails behind them.

Poetry stood there, me and the lamb beside and in front of him, with one of his fat hands resting on the top of the lamb's poll, and he looked down at it like it was his best friend or something and said to it, "Little innocent lamb, you'd make a very innocent white ghost next Friday night."

With that Poetry looked at me, winked and put

64

a fat forefinger up to his pursed lips. Then we both realized that Miss Lilly was standing at the school door, holding it open for us to hurry up and get through before we were too late.

Well, I got busy and found out how much Mr. Brown's lumber bill was so he could pay it. The afternoon moved along slowly, and I realized that is was going to be a slow week, 'cause I wanted next Friday night to come right that very minute so I could take my blanket and some kind of a pillow and sleep in the Sugar Creek cave.

At half-past two in the afternoon of that Monday at school, we had recess, which lasts only fifteen very short minutes that seem like only about five. As soon as I got a chance I talked to Big Jim alone. I said to him, "How come Sylvia's little sister Jeanelle gave the note to you? Where'd she get it and who wrote it?" Of course I knew Dragonfly had written it—printed it, rather—'cause he had the indelible pencil on his teeth and he was the only one who was afraid of ghosts. Besides that very morning he had stood in front of our big school dictionary and looked up the word "ghost" for us.

Big Jim looked down at me with a blushed expression on his face and said, "Who *told* you that?"

"I saw her give it to you," I said.

Big Jim looked pretty funny for a minute; then he said, "If you *have* to know, I gave it to Sylvia

65

last night in church to see what she thought about it, and she sent it back with Jeanelle this morning."

We were standing by ourselves under the big ash tree. The rest of the school, including even the girls, were up at the other end of the yard playing prisoner's base and hollering and making a lot of ordinary noise.

"Where'd you get the note in the first place?" I asked.

And he said, "Dragonfly gave it to me."

Just that minute there was a sound of somebody sneezing behind the tree. I looked and a part of Poetry was showing on one side of the big tree and the other side of him was showing on the other side, which shows how big the tree actually was. Big Jim looked around quick and that's how Poetry happened to get in on our talk. We had to invite him too, 'cause he'd heard us.

"And where did *Dragonfly* get the note?" Poetry asked. He winked at me secretly.

Big Jim said, "Little Jim gave it to him."

"*Little Jim!*" Poetry and I exclaimed in a duet.

"What's so funny about *that?*" Big Jim asked.

"Nothing," I said, "but where'd *Little Jim* get it?"

"Found it," Big Jim said and his face was sober. "Found it on their car floor."

66

"On their *car* floor!" Poetry and I exclaimed in another duet.

Just that minute the two-minute bell rang, which meant we'd all better get ready to make a dive for the schoolhouse door as soon as the last bell should ring, as it did almost right away.

As usual, Poetry and I walked and ran together, and just as we went whizzing past the lamb, he said to me, "Dragonfly didn't write that note."

"Why not?" I puffed.

" 'Cause Big Bob Till did."

I stopped running and walking, stood still and said, "Bob Till is still in Chicago, isn't he?" remembering the excitement we'd had there over Labor Day weekend which you already know about if you've read my other story about the Sugar Creek Gang in Chicago. I also remembered that Little Tom's brother, Big Bob Till, who had been arrested in Chicago, had been paroled to Little Jim's Dad.

Big Bob Till, you know, was the leader of a tough gang of town boys whom we'd licked the daylights out of last year in the famous battle of Bumblebee Hill near the old abandoned cemetery. Bob had stolen some money from our grocer's store, had run away to Chicago, had been arrested, and would have been in jail right that minute, I thought, if

Little Jim's Dad hadn't been willing to have him paroled to *him*.

"No," Poetry said just as we whizzed up to the roofless porch, "Big Bob came home Saturday afternoon in Little Jim's dad's car."

8

So! I THOUGHT. Big Bob Till is home again! The big ugly-faced boy whose father was an atheist and who hadn't been to church in his whole life, and who was always causing so much trouble for the Sugar Creek Gang, and who was the leader of the tough town gang of boys who called themselves "The Hellfire Gang."

All the rest of the afternoon, we kept thinking about him. I say "we" 'cause Poetry sent a note over to me and shouldn't have, and the note said:

> After school, let's go down to the cave and
> go in and listen again.

I folded the note quick and shoved it into one of my five pants pockets, just before Miss Lilly looked around from the blackboard where she had been working a problem for Dragonfly.

As soon as school was out and all the seventeen pupils had gone except Poetry and me, who stayed to sweep the floor and close the windows and finally to lock the door after Miss Lilly had gone; Poetry and I went down the lane to our house, with his pet lamb following and bringing its tail behind it.

"Home early, today?" Mom asked when I rushed into our kitchen to set my dinner pail on a shelf in the corner.

"Yep!" I said, "Poetry stayed and helped me so I could help him with something he wanted to do after school. Can I? I mean, can I go over to Poetry's house or somewhere to help him do something?"

Mom, who was sitting in the front room working on a very small dress for Charlotte Ann, looked up and talked with a pin in her mouth, "Why, yes, I guess so. Only your father is expecting you to take this shirt up to Old Man Paddler's cabin for him. He brought it to me this morning, saying you told him to. I've patched it the best I can."

Mom got up out of her sewing rocker and carefully wrapped Old Man Paddler's white shirt in a piece of paper and gave it to me. Mom had not only sewed up the jagged rip but had washed and ironed the shirt as well, which shows what kind of a mom I've got, and also how much she liked Old Man Paddler.

"Here," Mom said, "take these to him too." With that she went to our pantry to our cooky jar and took out two dozen fresh raisin cookies and gave them to me in a brown paper sack just as Poetry, who was on our back porch, cleared his husky throat.

"Why, hello, Poetry!" Mom exclaimed. "Would you like a cooky?"

"Of course, I mean, certainly. Thank you," Poetry said politely, always being especially polite at a time like that.

Well, it didn't take us long to get started through the woods to Old Man Paddler's house up in the hills, Poetry carrying the shirt and I the cookies.

We had to go past the old sycamore tree in order to get to the path that goes to Old Man Paddler's cottage, so when we got there we stopped at the cave to rest, 'cause the weather was still hot. We laid the cookies and the shirt in the hole in the tree, and both of us crawled slowly in through the cave entrance and sat down inside, the late afternoon sun shining in and making it almost light inside.

Just to give atmosphere, we lit one of the candles and then sat a while, noticing how nice and dry it was there, and what a fine place it was going to be for us to sleep next Friday night if our parents would let us.

We listened as hard as we could to see if we could hear the strange pounding noise we'd heard the day before, and we didn't—not at first. We did hear running water coming from somewhere, though,

71

but it was kind of faraway-sounding, and we decided maybe it was an underground stream somewhere. You know there are millions of little underground streams in the earth we live on, running everywhere and in different directions, like arteries and blood vessels running through a boy's body.

"Listen!" Poetry exclaimed squawkily into my ear, startling me. "Hear it? There it is again. That pounding noise!"

I listened, and sure enough there it was again, the same pounding we'd heard the day before, like somebody with a pickax digging away far back in the earth somewhere. I tell you I felt creepy, and the next thing we knew we were both outside, looking all around to see if we could see anybody or anything, and we couldn't. One thing I did see though with my mind's eye—that was the purple stains on Dragonfly's incisors, and I also in my imagination saw the crazily scribbled note which had told us the cave was haunted.

"I don't believe it!" Poetry said, and for the first time in a long time he had a worried expression on his face. "There isn't any such thing as a ghost!"

We listened outside and didn't hear anything, so we went inside again to blow out the candle.

"Maybe it was our imagination," I said.

Poetry said, "Absolutely not! I don't believe it anyway."

Just the same, it was spooky in that cave, so we got out, took our cookies and the shirt, and went on, Poetry carrying the cookies. Pretty soon while we walked and climbed the hill, he said, "How many cookies did you say there were in this sack?"

"Twenty-four," I answered. I'd seen Mom count them and put them all in a long row in the bottom of the sack.

"There's twenty-five," Poetry said, holding the sack open and looking in.

We walked on a while, and pretty soon he said, "Did you say there were supposed to be only twenty-four?"

"Maybe the ghost put an extra one in while we were in the cave," I said.

Poetry grunted and replied, "Any sensible ghost would have taken one out, rather than have put one in," and I agreed with him.

Just the same we had a tingling feeling inside, all the way up to Old Man Paddler's cabin, thinking and talking about what made the pounding noise, and wondering if it had been our imagination or not.

Just then Poetry stopped again, so very quick that I bumped right ker-squash into him. "Sh! Listen!"

I listened and there it was again, the same kind of a sound I'd heard before and it was right up ahead of us. In fact it was coming from the direction of Old Man Paddler's cabin.

Poetry and I looked at each other's face. Then we looked again at the cabin and there out in the back was the long-whiskered old man himself, chopping kindling on a big block of wood, which was on a big slab of rock behind his house.

That settled that, I thought, and so did Poetry. We hadn't heard any ghost, because there weren't any in the whole world.

"I'm *mad!*" Poetry exclaimed to me.

"Why?" I asked.

" 'Cause," Poetry answered. "I really wanted there to be a ghost—even if there isn't any such thing in the world."

Well, the minute that kind old man saw us coming, he straightened up, stood his ax against the block of wood on the big rock and said in his very kind old voice, "Good afternoon, Poetry. Good afternoon, Bill."

"We brought your shirt," I said, holding out the package toward one of his gnarled old hands.

Poetry said, "And two dozen cookies, from Bill's mom—I mean, from Mrs. Collins."

"Well, well," the old man said with sunshine in his voice. "Come on in the house a while, and I'll get you something to take back with you."

He carried the shirt in one hand and the sack of

cookies in the other. We followed him inside and sat down on a couple of wooden, homemade chairs, while Old Man Paddler walked to the trapdoor in the floor and lifted it up and went down into his cellar. The minute his white hair disappeared down in that dark hole, I remembered the time he had fallen down that same stairway himself the year before and had hurt his leg and would maybe have frozen to death if our gang hadn't come up to his cabin that day and saved his life. I remembered that it wasn't much of a cellar, just about ten feet square, and I was feeling proud of myself and the gang to think we'd saved his life, when just that minute Poetry who was sitting on half of his chair, jumped, lost his balance and went kersquash on the floor.

" 'Smatter?" I asked, and say, he was almost white.

He looked up at me and picked himself up off the floor, and said, "Did you *hear* that?" His voice had a husky whisper in it.

"Hear what?"

"A door slam shut!"

I looked at him and said, "So you're getting to be like Dragonfly! Scared of ghosts."

"I—I *a-am* not! But I *did* hear a door slam somewhere."

"What *of* it?" I said, scolding him. "Can't a door

slam without giving you the jitters? That was the wind maybe, blowing the woodshed door shut."

I looked out the window, and the woodshed door was wide open and propped open with a stick, and besides the wind wasn't blowing.

Just that minute Old Man Paddler's white head and long white beard came up the cellar steps, and he had in one hand a little box full of reddish-colored pieces of wood that looked like a lot of chips from our woodpile at home.

Sassafras roots, I thought, remembering that Little Jim always likes sassafras tea so well.

Mr. Paddler shut the trapdoor, with both of us watching and helping a little, and then he said, "If you aren't in a hurry, I'll make you some tea, and we can have a little tea party with your cookies."

But we were supposed to be in a hurry, so he didn't urge us to stay. He opened the paper sack of cookies though and put them on a plate, and put the sassafras roots in the paper bag for me to take home, half of the roots being for Poetry's parents and the other half for mine. I counted the cookies while he was taking them out, and there were exactly twenty-four, like my mom had said there were in the first place. "You're arithmetic is getting worse," I said to Poetry. "There are just twenty-four. You can't count straight."

And he grinned and said, "I'm still good at subtraction," then he grinned again and started whistling to himself. I never did find out what he meant or why he had that mischievous look in his eyes.

The minute we got out the door and started down the little hill following the old man's path to the spring where he gets his drinking water, Poetry turned around real quick and said, "Mr. Paddler, do you believe in ghosts?"

9

WELL, WE MIGHT have known the old man didn't believe in ghosts, or disembodied spirits hanging around this world, making pounding noises in caves or slamming doors. He explained why he didn't believe in them, and we started on home, following the winding old wagontrail partway, and then cutting off and going through the swamp to save time. Just as we started to disappear in the thick woods, we heard a car coming in low gear up the trail. Looking down we saw a beautiful green coupé and we knew right away whose it was.

"Miss Lilly!" Poetry and I exclaimed under our breaths and ducked down behind some second-growth oaks to hide until the car went purring past.

"What's she doing going up to Old Man Paddler's?" Poetry asked me.

"I don't know," I said, but I felt myself liking both of them at the same time, thinking maybe if she had been his daughter, she would have had a very nice father. Then Poetry and I hurried on, stopping for a jiffy at the cave and listening but not hearing anything, and finally hurrying on to

Poetry's house, each one of us thinking and talking and feeling fine because we did not believe there was any such thing as a ghost and tickled that we were going to sleep in the cave that Friday night, if our parents would let us.

"We must not tell our folks we think we've heard anything," I said to Poetry, "or they'll be afraid to let us sleep there."

"Or else they'll laugh at us for being superstitious," Poetry panted to me. We'd been running hard for a minute 'cause we felt so good, when we stopped at his gate to get our breath.

"There just isn't any sense to what we thought we heard," Poetry said, and there wasn't.

Well, it was time for me to go home and help Dad with the chores, so I told Poetry, "So long," which means, "Good-bye for a while," or else it means, "It will be just *so* long until we see each other again."

It was while I was up in our haymow throwing down forkfuls of alfalfa hay for our horses and cows that I heard my Dad downstairs talking to somebody, so I listened, and it was Old Man Paddler.

How in the world! I thought. How did he get here so quick? Why that old man had to walk with a cane and he certainly couldn't walk as fast as Poetry and I could—although I suppose I did get home a little later because I had stopped at Poetry's house. Of course he could have ridden with Miss Lilly, in her car, I thought.

"No," my dad's big half-gruff voice said, "I don't think there is any use to try. The law is the law and that settles it. I do hate to see a boy have to go to the reformatory for his first offense though."

Then Old Man Paddler's trembling old voice came floating up to me kind of like a screech owl's voice does at night as he said, "I keep thinking, what if it was my William that was in trouble?"

"I know—I know," Dad's big voice answered, and then my dad said something that made me feel creepy all over, and made me wonder what was going to happen. It also made me a little bit angry. My dad said, "Well, I'll have a talk with him and see if I can get him to change his ways."

What! I thought. *Are they talking about me?*

"Thank you, Mr. Collins," Old Man Paddler said. "That will help, I am sure. Maybe it's just a whim of an old man, but I believe it's worth trying. Some of the world's greatest men have been made of bad-boy material. If I remember right, you were active yourself when you were only a little red-haired—" Then the old man's voice was lost just as one of our cows, who had lost her calf the day before, let out a very sorrowful bawl.

I stood there feeling hot inside, and worried, and wondering what I'd done wrong, and I couldn't think of anything except the lamb at school and my having given the woodshed key to Poetry and helping him to do his mischievous prank.

Both my dad's voice and Old Man Paddler's were getting fainter so I knew they were walking away. I peeped through a crack between the weatherboarding of the barn and saw them walking toward our house, my dad's bushy reddish-brown hair and the old man's white hair side by side, with the going-down sun shining on them.

They stopped right under the crossbeam that goes over our grape arbor, near our iron pitcher pump, and my grayish-brown-haired mom came out with her blue apron on and stood there with her hands on her hips like a person sometimes does when he is angry about something and is trying to decide what to do about it.

I *wished*—how I *wished* I could have heard what they were saying about me, but I couldn't. Anyway, I thought maybe Miss Lilly had told my parents about the lamb at school or maybe something else I'd done, which I couldn't think of, and I began to imagine all kinds of things going to happen to me.

I was down on my knees there on the alfalfa, looking out of the crack of the barn and listening to pigeons cooing from up high in the rafters somewhere, and I felt very worried. Well, maybe you wouldn't be interested to know what I did then, but I said a few words to my *very* best Friend, whom I was beginning to like very much 'cause He was all the time *with* me, and always let me know when I had done right or wrong. He was helping me to swim upstream against the current and everything. I know that He knew I hadn't done anything actually wrong on purpose, and I also knew He would understand a boy's mind.

All of a sudden, while I was still peeping through the crack in the barn and looking at the big round, red sun that was going down, that looked like a big red globe, I remembered the globe on Miss Lilly's desk; and I could see one of her pretty white hands on the top of the world and the other white hand on the top of the lamb's head. I remembered what she said, and without hardly knowing it, I said out loud to myself, "Behold the Lamb of God that taketh away Bill Collins' sins." Then as quick as a flash, I was standing up again and starting to throw down more hay, when I heard my mom's cheerful voice calling me to supper.

Boy, oh boy! There is something wonderful about the way a boy's mom's voice sounds when it comes waving across the barnyard to tell you supper is ready. You begin to smell raw-fried potatoes right away, and you can even see the table before you get there. You can see your plate set with the silverware placed just right, with your big blue mug filled with rich cold milk standing in its place; and there will be steaming wonderful-smelling potatoes, bread and butter, a salad of some kind and maybe a piece of cold blackberry pie left over from dinner.

That is, you feel like that if everything is all right between you and your parents. When I got down out of the haymow, I saw Old Man Paddler standing by our front gate, and Miss Lilly's car was there again. Miss Lilly waved at me, and I tipped my straw hat to her, and even Old Man Paddler turned around and said, "Hello, Bill." Then he climbed in her car and they drove off down the road. A jiffy later, when I was in our bathroom washing the day's different kinds of dirt off my hands and face and neck and ears even, I heard the boards rumbling on the Sugar Creek bridge and I knew it was Miss Lilly's automobile with Old Man Paddler in it going toward Tom and Bob Till's house, and I wondered why.

Pretty soon we were all sitting down at the table with Charlotte Ann sitting up in her high chair between me and Mom, and Dad sitting straight across the table from us.

That supper smelled so good, I was about to forget what I was worried about, until Dad's prayer asking the blessing started me to feeling bothered again. He said, in his big voice which had a sad note in it, "Please, heavenly Father, bless the boys of the Sugar Creek Gang and keep them from all harm and danger. Bless our own son with his many temptations and problems and—"

The second he said problems, my thoughts were back in our little red brick schoolhouse thinking of Mr. Brown's sheep and of his lumber bill and how many pounds of wool his many sheep had, of Poetry's lamb and of how it acted when it was in school, of the key to the woodshed door, which I'd given Poetry, of Miss Lilly and Old Man Paddler and of a reformatory and everything else.

My thoughts came back to Dad's prayer just as he finished by saying, "And help Mother and me to be the right kind of parents, so we shall be able to stand unashamed before Thee at Thy coming again. For Jesus' sake, Amen."

Say, things must have been happening fast around Sugar Creek, I thought, for something unusual was going on. Just about the minute we were half through eating, there was another car at our front gate and this time it was Mr. Foote, Little Jim's dad. He came hurrying across the yard, like he was excited about something, and the first thing I knew he was at the door.

Right away I thought of Bob Till who had been paroled to him or was supposed to have been, and

I thought of the crazy note written in indelible pencil that Little Jim had found on the floor of his dad's car.

We finished supper right away and I went out to the car where Little Jim was sitting down, or rather he was standing up in our big swing under the walnut tree pumping himself up and down, while Mom and Dad and Mr. Foote talked to each other about something—what, I didn't know. But I *did* know that Mr. Foote was the township trustee and that sometimes when boys made trouble in school the teachers had had to send them to him to get a good talking to.

Things looked bad and I was worried.

"Hi, Little Jim," I said sadly.

"What are you so sad about?" he asked, pumping himself higher.

"Nothing," I said. "Does your dad know about the lamb at school?"

Little Jim stopped pumping his knees and said, "I'm going to stay at your house tonight."

"Why?" I said.

" 'Cause my parents are going away somewhere."

"Why?" I said, and then remembered Little Jim hadn't answered my other question, so I asked it again, "Does your dad know about my—about the lamb at school?"

Say, that little guy looked kind of sad at my ques-

tions, and he said, "I don't know—I don't guess so."
Just that minute Charlotte Ann started to cry about
something in the house and Little Jim lifted his
feet up, his small hands holding onto the ropes on
each side of the swing, and then he let himself sit
down on the board seat kerplop. "What's *that?*"

"Oh, *that!*" I said. "That's Charlotte Ann crying."

"I wish I had a little baby sister," he said wist-
fully.

Little Jim and I went over to his car then, and he
showed me the very spot on the back floor of his
car where he'd found the note that had been written in indelible pencil.

"Where's Bob Till now?" I asked.

"Nobody knows," Little Jim said and looked
sad. "He's run away and now if he gets arrested,
he'll have to go to reformatory from one to ten
years, Father says." Little Jim always called his
dad "Father," which is a very respectful name, although it didn't mean he liked him any better than
I did my dad, even though I called mine by a
shorter name. My dad was not only my *dad,* but
he was my pal also. I not only obeyed him, but I
also played games with him, such as, checkers in
the wintertime, or carrom, or something, and base-
ball in the summer; and when we worked together,

we made a game of it and had lots of fun, making the hard work seem like play.

Pretty soon, Mr. Foote came out and drove away. Little Jim and I carried his little suitcase into our house and up to my room. Then we helped Dad finish the chores and later went up to bed, neither of us knowing what important things were going to happen during the night.

10

ONE OF THE IMPORTANT THINGS that happened was the grandest thing that could ever have happened to Little Jim. His being the littlest member of our gang had always bothered him and made him feel as if he wasn't very important.

Just after he and I had crawled into my great big bed with the clean, fresh-smelling sheets on it, my dad's big steps started coming up the stairs. My dad nearly always did that—had been doing it ever since I was little—coming up to say goodnight and to tell me a short story, or read me one, or quote a poem or a hymn or something. When I was even littler than little, Mom had taught me to say my prayer at night and had always tucked me in, but Dad nearly always liked to have a final look at me to see if I was all right, to see if I had any scratches or bruises or sore toes or black eyes or anything that might need attention of some kind.

Well, Dad's big heavy-soled leather shoes always sounded good coming up, so Little Jim and I lay there listening and waiting in the dark, having blown the lamp out a jiffy before, and tumbled into bed, each one of us having said his prayers quietly on his knees beside the bed.

I couldn't even see Dad at first, 'cause I was still used to the light. Then when he cleared his throat, he was so close to us it sounded kind of like a big bear growling—Grrrrrr! Garumph!

"Any bumps?" Dad asked.

"Nope!" I said.

"Any scratches needing merthiolate?"

"Nope," I said into my pillow.

"Any cuts or bruises or black eyes or smashed noses or bee stings or wood ticks that need to be pulled off? Or dirty feet that need washing or—?"

Little Jim's giggle interrupted him, and Dad said to him, "Little Jim, we're proud to have you for Bill's friend. You boys want to hear a poem or something?"

With that my dad started to quote what had been one of my favorite poems, which was in a hymn in our hymnbook and had been written—the music, I mean—by Sankey, an evangelistic singer who used to travel with a man named Dwight L. Moody. The poem in Dad's gruff kind of dramatic voice went like this:

> There were ninety and nine that safely lay
> In the shelter of the fold,

But one was out on the hills away,
    Far off from the gates of gold;
Away on the mountains wild and bare,
    Away from the tender Shepherd's care.
Lord, Thou hast here Thy ninety and nine;
    Are they not enough for Thee?
But the Shepherd made answer: This of Mine
    Has wandered away from Me.

On and on my dad's voice went, and I went out on the wings of his voice and looked all around through the mountains and hills and in the desert and among the thorns to help find the one lost sheep, which finally the Shepherd found; and I even climbed up on the shoulders of the Good Shepherd and rode along with the little found sheep, only I guess maybe I was the sheep myself.

It was a great poem, and Dad finished it grandly, standing there in the dark with one hand on the post of the bedstead.

All of a sudden Little Jim piped up like a small frog and asked—his small voice right close to my right ear—"Is Jesus the Good Shepherd as well as the Lamb of God?"

And Dad said, "Yes."

When morning came, and we were on our way to school, Little Jim having his lunch packed with mine in my basket, Little Jim was the happiest little guy you ever saw, 'cause the night before, while he was at our house, and his parents were away from home, in town in fact, Little Jim got a brand-new baby sister, and he could go to see her that very day after school, his mother being in a hospital.

"What's her name?" Dragonfly wanted to know right away just like he does whenever any of the gang gets a new sister or something. We were at the big tall iron pump not far from the gray school-house door with the white knob on it, when Dragonfly asked the question.

Little Jim already knew the answer, 'cause my mom had already been to see the baby, so he said proudly, "Her name is Jill Nadene."

Dragonfly frowned and said, trying to be funny, "I'll bet she's only about a Foote long."

And Poetry whose parents had also already been to see the baby, came puffing up just then and said,

> Little Jim and Jill went up the hill
> To fetch a pail of water;
> Jim fell down and broke his crown,
> And Jill came tumbling after.

"It's a pretty name," I said to Little Jim, remembering what he'd said last year when my little sister was born, and I'd told him her name was Charlotte Ann.

"Sure it is!" Little Jim said. I looked at him, as

he stood standing straight beside the sugar tree, and he actually looked like he had grown several inches during the night, just like a stalk of corn does when it's had a good rain. Little Jim's having a baby sister to protect was like a good rain to make him grow. He looked bigger. He even felt bigger, which a boy does at a time like that.

He, Dragonfly, Poetry and I all went inside the school to see that the dust was all off the seats, the windows were open and the blackboard was clean— which it wasn't very long because Poetry and Little Jim started playing tictacktoe on it. Dragonfly went back to his new hobby, which was looking up words in the dictionary.

Seeing Dragonfly standing there like that, I said to him, "Look up the word 'superstitious,' will you?" and he did. It was, "Disposed to believe in superstitions," which didn't make much sense to our minds, but whatever it was it wasn't a compliment to be that. And Dragonfly was *it*.

Well, in a little while others of the seventeen children started to come and after a while we were all in our seats again with Miss Lilly standing in her nice dress with the lily designs on it, looking out over the room at us, smiling and also looking sober.

We came to order, and then she said, "Boys and girls of district No. 9"—which is the number of our

93

district in Sugar Creek township—"I have a serious problem to present to you. As you know, Mr. Foote, our township trustee, has been instrumental in securing the release of—" Miss Lilly's blue eyes roved the room for a minute and focused on Little Tom Till, then hurried on to me and the rest of us, as she went on saying—"the release from boy's jail, of Robert Till. Robert came home Saturday afternoon, and then as suddenly disappeared again, which means of course, that he has done what is called 'jumped parole' or violated his parole. That means plenty of trouble for him, at least a longer sentence for him in the reformatory.

"Now!" Miss Lilly looked so very pretty standing there beside her desk, that I got to thinking about spiders again and wished I could kill one for her. "Now," she said, "what Mr. Paddler and I are trying to do is to give him still another chance, and we need your cooperation. Robert is afraid to come home and live here now, because he says everybody will make fun of him and have nothing to do with him. Now, I have here a paper which I'd like you all to sign, and as soon as we find Robert, we'll let him read it. Perhaps he will come back to school again and continue his education. All boys need an education—almost *have* to have it in these days."

Pretty soon Miss Lilly's nice speech was finished and she walked straight across to Big Jim on the other side of the room to ask him to sign first. She had just read us the petition and it was:

> We, the undersigned members of district No. 9, Sugar Creek Township, want Robert Till to have another chance. We pledge ourselves not to make fun of him or at any time say anything to make him feel humiliated. We will treat him like one of the rest of us, if he will come back to school.

Say, Big Jim didn't bat an eye, but just sat there staring at the paper lying on his desk and at Miss Lilly's gold fountain pen which she was holding out for him to sign with. Big Jim's hands were under his desk with his fists doubled up. I'd seen those same doubled-up fists before in the battle of Bumblebee Hill when both of them had gone *ker-whack, ker-smash, ker-squash, ker-bang-bang-bang-bang*-WHAM! against Bob Till's face and side and nose and jaw, paying Big Bob back blow for blow, fighting in self-defense, and also fighting what is called an offensive battle, which my dad says is the best defense. I'd seen those same Big Jim fists— one of them—after he had split the knuckles open on a bank robber's jaw once. Also in Chicago I'd seen one of his arms, naked and stretched out with a hollow needle in one of the veins, and had seen the red blood of Big Jim flowing out to save Big Bob's life, by giving a transfusion.

Now as I looked, I saw the muscles on Big Jim's jaw working. I knew he knew Big Bob was his worst enemy and that Bob hated him like poison and would do anything—any low-down trick to get the best of Big Jim. And Big Jim was supposed to sign that paper!

Say, Big Jim just sat there, still staring at the paper, and not *taking* the pen which Miss Lilly was holding out to him. I tell you his face looked grim and his lips were pressed firmly together. I knew he liked Miss Lilly and would maybe do anything in the world to please her if he could, but— well, what *was* he going to do? Sign or not?

Then Big Jim looked at me, and his steel-blue eyes were set and hard, and also kind of sad. He looked around the room and then back again to the paper and I thought he had made up his mind to sign, which if he did, all the rest of us would. Then just as quick as a chipmunk along Sugar Creek can make an almost invisible movement when he picks up a nut or something to eat, Big Jim's writing hand reached out for the pen.

I sighed with relief, 'cause I felt sorry for Bob Till in spite of his meanness and his swearing, foul-mouthed dad. I felt especially sorry for his sad-faced mother who had never had a chance to be happy, and never would have unless things were changed, or unless she let the One who had made

96

her come into her life and make her happy inside, as my mom once told me.

But say, Big Jim wasn't signing that paper! He had the pen in his hand all right, then in both hands, and the next jiffy, with his eyes still staring at the paper or else at his desk in front of him, he took the cap off the end of the pen, slowly screwed it onto the other end, where the pen point was, and looking up at Miss Lilly with his face set, he said, "I'm sorry, Miss Lilly. The Sugar Creek Gang can't sign that paper. We'd like to, but we can't!" He made a quick gesture with the closed pen and handed it back to her.

11

THE SUGAR CREEK GANG can't sign that paper!"

That's what my unbelieving ears had heard Big Jim, our leader, say.

The atmosphere in that room was thick as smoke for a while, until Miss Lilly sort of came to herself, probably feeling as if Big Jim had struck her. She stood in front of his desk with the pen in her hand and with a hurt expression on her face; then she turned to the rest of us, kind of like a fish that was out of the water gasping for air and like she wanted us to sympathize with her or something.

She picked up the paper from Big Jim's desk, went up and laid it on her own, and to all of us she said in a friendly voice, "Let us all be thankful that we live in America, a country where men and women and children can be free to follow the dictates of their own consciences, without being compelled by some dictator." Then she smiled in every direction, even in Big Jim's direction and announced, "Will the first grade reading class please pass?" and all the little girls in the small front seats scrambled from different directions and went up to the

99

front bench which is called a "recitation" bench, and the rest of us got busy on our own work.

My very first arithmetic problem was about a grocer who was counting the money in his cash register, and I couldn't help but think of Bob Till again, 'cause that was the reason he was in trouble in the first place—he had broken into our grocer's, Mr. Simondson's store, and taken some money out of the cash register, and Big Jim had seen him break in, which was through a back door in an alley.

Anyway, Miss Lilly didn't say anything more about the paper, and we didn't either, although I noticed that Big Jim all of a sudden, when it was recess and he saw Miss Lilly starting to pump herself a drink at the long-handled iron pump, jumped and ran lickety-sizzle across the schoolyard to the pump and offered to pump the water for her. She let him do it, and said, "Thank you, Jim." She also smiled at him.

That day passed, and the next and the next, but nobody saw Bob Till, and nobody said anything to us about him. He had just dropped out of sight like a hole had opened in the earth and he had fallen in and disappeared.

Then came Friday night when Dragonfly saw the ghost, which we saw ourselves too.

It had been a simple matter to convince our parents to let us sleep in the cave that Friday night. Of course some of our dads had gone down to look at it and to go inside and see how dry it was and that it had safe walls and a safe ceiling that wouldn't cave in.

I had my outdoor sleeping bag all ready and my night clothes, 'cause even though we were going to sleep in a cave, I had to wear pajamas. I walked into our living room after supper, and took a look at Charlotte Ann who was asleep in her bassinet. She had one cute little fist doubled up and pressed against her nose and the other was down under some blankets or somewhere. She was lying on her side breathing noisily and fast like babies do when they're asleep.

"Well, little sister," I said, "you're still too small to know what it is to be a man and sleep out in the wilds." Then I turned around and looked toward our kitchen to say "Good-bye" to Mom, who turned away quick with a funny smile on her face and a small chuckle in her voice.

" 'Smatter?" I asked. "What's so funny?"

"Everything's fine, Billy-boy." She picked up a chair and moved it over against the kitchen wall, then straightened a curtain, finally went into the bathroom, turned on a faucet and got herself a drink.

At the kitchen door I stopped, turned around and said, "Well—?"

Mom didn't say anything, but set the glass she had been drinking out of in its place.

"Well," I said, wondering why she didn't say anything, "I'm going away for the night."

"What time will you want breakfast?" Mom asked. "Or will you boys eat at the cave?"

Say, she didn't seem to realize how important it was for me to sleep away from home in a dangerous cave, just like a wild man, so I said, "Oh, maybe about half-past seven."

"We'll have it at seven as usual," Mom said, and went on working.

Outdoors, I called to Dad who was at the barn, and said, "Good night, Dad, I'm going now."

He looked up. In his hand was a pail of mixed skim milk and bran which he had been pouring out into a long hog trough where about seventeen pigs were trying to eat out of a trough only long enough for twelve.

"So long, Bill," Dad hollered back to me, and turned to his work.

"So long," I called back, and just that minute Dragonfly came whizzing up to our gate on his bicycle, and also just that minute Dad said, "I'll leave the back door open, Bill, in case for any reason you decide you'd rather sleep the rest of the night in your own warm, safe bed."

That made me angry. Imagine my dad thinking I'd be *scared* of anything, or couldn't rough it, or wouldn't be *safe* in an innocent cave!

"Hello, Dragonfly," I said, "Ready?"

"Mom won't let me."

"Won't let you what?" I asked.

"Mom won't let me sleep in the cave."

"I thought you said your dad said you *could*," I said.

And Dragonfly said, "I have *two* parents, and Mom says the cave is too close to the cemetery."

"Too close to a place where there are a lot of dead people?" It was disgusting to hear talk like that. "You're too superstitious," I said. "That's what you get for studying the dictionary so much. You know there isn't any such thing as a ghost—and—"

"*You* know it and *I* know it, but my *mother* doesn't know it," Dragonfly said, the same thing he was always saying. "There was a great big black cat ran right across the road in front of me less than six minutes ago," he finished.

"He probably *ran* because he was afraid of you," I said, kidding him—anyway trying to.

"But doesn't that mean bad luck?"

"Only to people who are dumb enough to believe it," I told him.

Well, the cave was on the way to Dragonfly's house, as was the old abandoned cemetery, so I had to ride on to his house with him on the handlebars of his bike to help him convince the other side of his parents that it was perfectly safe for a strong boy to sleep in an innocent cave.

When we got to Dragonfly's house, his mom was worried as anything. "You boys aren't really going to try to sleep in that old cave, are you?" she asked, and I looked at her worried face.

"Certainly," I said politely, "and I've come to ask special permission for Dragonfly. We need him. He's almost the most important member of the gang. Besides," I said, "there isn't any such thing as a ghost—Old Man Paddler says so."

Dragonfly's mom was just taking a pie out of the oven, so she set it on the table on a breadboard and said, slowly, "Well, I suppose I'll have to let him go. Would you like a piece of blueberry pie?"

Well, that settled that. We ate the pie. It also settled something else in my mind, 'cause when we got through eating that pie, Dragonfly's teeth looked like they had indelible pencil stains on them.

Pretty soon Dragonfly's mom had his blanket ready for him and his night clothes, and we rode away. At the end of their lane all of a sudden a big black cat darted out from behind their hedge and tried to dash across the road in front of us. Dragonfly and I were both on the bike, and the cat and all of us got tangled up. He stepped on the brakes quick, skidded the back tire, and we both turned upside down in the ditch, on top of each other and the bicycle and also of the cat, which hissed and beat it in some direction or other.

"What did I tell you?" Dragonfly cried from under me somewhere, and I answered from somewhere under *him* and the bicycle, "It wasn't the cat's fault. It's only people that believe in superstitious things that have accidents like this and get banged up."

"Do *you* believe in them?" Dragonfly asked, which was a sarcastic question.

The bicycle was still all right, so we got up and rode on. We left the bike not far from the cave and got there ahead of some of the gang. Big Jim and Circus were already there, arranging things, driving a stick or two in the cracks in the wall for us to hang our clothes on.

It wasn't dark yet—not quite—and there were several hundred dozen mosquitoes which would want to eat us up if they could, so we gathered firewood. After a while we'd have a fire to help keep the mosquitoes away.

In a short while Little Jim Foote and Poetry came along. Little Tom Till couldn't come, because his parents would not let him. We were all sitting around the mouth of the cave and talking and looking into the fire which we had built against a rock not far from the entrance.

Time flew past too fast. Soon it was nine o'clock, and time to go to bed. We sat around inside, with the two candles lit, one on a shelf on one side and one on the other, and the firelight making us feel sure there wouldn't be any wild animal out there that would dare to try to get in.

Big Jim took out his New Testament and read to us a fine chapter from the book of John. The story was about a fire that the Lord Himself had built on the shore of Lake Galilee one morning, and how the Lord and Peter had a talk about how much Peter loved Him. I felt myself wishing I had been Peter and had loved the Lord like he did. I even wished maybe sometime I'd get to see Jesus just like He looked when He was here on earth.

After that each one said his own prayers, most of us saying them quietly, and then we were ready to go to sleep.

We drew straws to see who got to blow the candles out, and Poetry and I got the job, which we did in two breaths at the same time just like we'd done it before.

Then we lay down, and as quick, Dragonfly was squirming and saying, "Ouch! What in the world?"

" 'Smatter?" most of us whispered to him and told him to keep still.

"I'm lying on something hard. I can feel it through my blanket."

I turned on my flashlight and he dug down under him and pulled something out, and would you believe it? It was a cuff link like Old Man Paddler used in his shirts.

"How'd that get here?" he asked. Imagine a cuff link in a cave!

By that time we were all sitting up in different directions blinking our eyes and looking at the cuff link and at each other.

"Aw, that's nothing to get worried about," Poetry said sleepily, but he nudged me and put his fat forefinger up to his lips, which meant "Sh!" "It might have gotten tangled up in some of our clothes, and we brought it from home. Let's get back to sleep."

With that remark and explanation, which seemed to satisfy all of us, Poetry turned back to his blanket. I snapped my flashlight off again, and we all were trying to sleep again.

Just as I was about to doze and after everybody else seemed like he was asleep, I felt Poetry nudge me gently and whisper real close to my ear, *"Psst,* Bill. Are you awake?"

I was, but I didn't want to be, I was so sleepy.

" 'Smatter?" I asked.

And he whispered, "Feel this?" He shoved something into my hand, and I could feel right away what it was. It was a little bottle, like the kind Charlotte Anne used to use, with a nipple on it and was what Poetry had used to get his lamb to follow him to school that Monday morning.

"What in the world?" I thought, but got my thoughts interrupted, when Poetry whispered to me, "There's a ghost tied out there in the bushes waiting for you and me to go and get it."

12

I STILL DIDN'T WANT to wake up, but Poetry was already fumbling himself out of his blanket and crawling toward the cave's exit; so I did the same thing, and the next thing we knew we were both far enough outside not to be heard by anybody. I wasn't interested in being mischievous at that time of night, but Poetry had everything all planned to half scare the daylights out of the gang, so I had to listen to him.

Say, as soon as we were far enough away, we turned on our flashlights, and pretty soon we found the lamb. It was tied to a small tree not very far from the cave. Poetry had a sheet under his arm, which I hadn't noticed before, and right away he started to wrap it around the lamb.

By that time I was wide awake and ready for the fun, although his idea still wasn't clear to me. "What are you going to do? How you goin' to make a ghost out of an innocent lamb?"

"Easy," he whispered, already working to get the nose of the lamb through the hole made for it.

"Now," Poetry puffed, looking something like a ghost himself in his flapping pajamas. "We'll tie you, Jerry-boy," Poetry said in a friendly voice to the lamb, "right behind the sycamore, and the rest will be easy."

Well, it *was* easy. We tied the ridiculous looking lamb to the sycamore tree, and crawled back slowly to the cave. At the entrance, we stopped low, listened and didn't hear anything and for a broken second Poetry turned his flashlight on the lamb. Say, I almost jumped out of my green pajamas, the way that lamb looked, with his big eyes staring into the light, and with the absolutely grotesque white clothes, with its eyeholes and its noseholes and a long white tail, and also the white horns Poetry had made for it.

I don't know what Poetry's plan was for after that, for just that second his innocent lamb let out a mournful bleat, and then another and another, and tried to get loose from itself.

Behind us we heard noises and the rest of the gang waking up and talking. I saw flashlights going on, and the fun had started.

Poetry and I darted back behind something or other and turned our flashlights on the crazy-acting lamb, and also watched the gang come crawling and tumbling out of the cave.

Talk about ghosts! They certainly looked ridiculous as I turned my flashlight on them for only a half jiffy. Big Jim with his purple pajamas on, Little Jim with his half-a-dozen-colored ones, Circus with his white, short ones that were so short they came halfway to his knees and almost to his elbows, Dragonfly with his striped ones, the stripes running around instead of up and down, and all of them, or most of them rubbing their eyes and looking at the lamb like they were seeing a ghost.

I tell you there was plenty of excitement around there for a few jiffies. As soon as the gang found out it was a trick, they were all set to take Poetry and me down to Sugar Creek and duck us, pajamas and all, but the lamb interrupted their plans. Say, with all that noise it got terribly scared. It bleated pitifully and was so afraid that Big Jim took things in his own hands and said, "That lamb has got to go home to its mother."

Well, as you know, Poetry lived closer to the old sycamore tree than any of the rest of us, so it didn't take us long to get started taking the lamb home. Big Jim made us do it, saying the little thing would probably be scared half to death, if we didn't. So he and the rest of us took it, Poetry taking off the ridiculous suit first. Then Big Jim said, "Get your pants and shoes on, all of you, and follow me—*all* of you!" he finished his command sternly.

Pretty soon we were walking along toward Poetry's pasture where there would be other lambs and sheep. I followed right behind Big Jim, holding my flashlight for him to see, and noticing the lamb as he carried it on his shoulder in the way a farmer does who knows how to carry a lamb and all the time I was thinking about the "Ninety-and-Nine," and looking at the little lamb. Once as we trudged along, I reached out my hand and put it on the lamb's withers, and the poor little thing was trembling like it was cold and terribly afraid.

I could see Poetry was sorry, for he had a very tender heart for animals and wouldn't hurt one for anything, that being one reason why he had been able to make the lamb a pet in the first place.

It was when we were on our way back to the cave that the thing happened—that Dragonfly saw the real ghost. It was nearer to go past Bumblebee Hill to get back to the cave than any other way. We decided to go that way even though the old cemetery was at the top, so we did. It was still not later than ten o'clock, but it was pretty chilly for that time of night, and the dew was on the grass, making us glad we all had our pajamas covered or they'd have been wet at the cuffs and we'd have had to sleep that way later on. For a minute I remembered Dad's words to come home and sleep in my own nice, warm bed if I wanted to, but I wouldn't have done it for the world.

We came to Bumblebee Hill and started to go across it, and were about halfway, right close to the place where I'd once smashed Little Tom's nose in the fight we'd had there, when all of a sudden Dragonfly stopped dead still and said, "Psst! Listen," which we all did, some of us bumping into the ones in front of us who had stopped quicker than *we* had.

"Look!" Dragonfly hissed. "There goes that lamb, running toward the cemetery."

We looked up, and that's exactly what it did look like, away up there at the top.

"How in the world!" Poetry said. We had opened their gate at their farm and put it inside, and here it was out and running, only not toward *us*, but in a different direction.

Well, we gave chase, and all started to run toward the top. We turned our flashlights on it, but it had already disappeared over the fence. In almost a half minute the seven of us were at the top of the hill, going through the fence right at the place where Old Man Paddler had torn his shirt the Sunday before.

It was Dragonfly who stopped us. "Hey!" he cried, when we had all gone through. I turned around and there he was, in his prison pajamas, standing on the other side. "I—I—I'm scared! There might be a *real* ghost! Hey! *Hey!* There is one!

LOOK!" He shouted in a scream that was smothered in fear.

We looked in every direction and finally saw something white streaking out across the cemetery, past Old Man Paddler's wife's grave, and moaning and running, or moving or flying or something. Then it started beating it for Sugar Creek and toward the cave.

That settled that! It wasn't any innocent lamb! It was an honest-to-goodness ghost, of which there weren't any.

"AFTER HIM!" Big Jim ordered.

And we were after him—even Dragonfly, getting up a little bravery from the rest of us. Being brave is contagious, you know. You follow the leader if *he* is brave, and you aren't scared unless *he* is, which Big Jim wasn't. Or else you can be scared and brave at the same time, which is the way I felt.

Lickety-sizzle, dodge, plunge, rush, hurry, dash, fall-down-get-up-quick, plunge on—that's the way we six boys tore through our woods after that white ghost, with our minds made up to catch whatever it was.

"Look!" Dragonfly puffed from somewhere among us, "It's going straight for the cave!" which it was.

My flashlight showed me the cave almost fifty feet ahead of us and then the ghost or whatever it was—we didn't know—stumbled over a log and down it went ker-plop right in front of the cave. Big Jim, who was in the lead with Circus right behind him and me next, got there almost at the same time; and the next thing we knew, Big Jim had made a head-first tackle like he does in a football game and he and the ghost were on the ground together, scrambling and wrestling. The ghost was panting and fighting like everything, and then all of a sudden it worked itself loose from Big Jim. There was a ripping and a tearing as Big Jim held onto some of its clothes, and the next thing we knew, the ghost or whatever it was was gone and Big Jim stood there, holding in his hands a great big white torn shirt.

"It went inside the cave!" Dragonfly hissed, and it had.

Well, I tell you, you can talk about excitement. There just never was anything like that ever happened. It couldn't even be so, I thought. I was merely having a crazy dream 'cause I was trying to sleep in a cave, and yet it wasn't a dream because right there in front of my eyes was a torn white shirt in Big Jim's hands, and—

Say! All of a sudden Poetry said, "There's your other cuff link, Dragonfly, in the cuff of that shirt."

I knew ghosts weren't supposed to wear shirts with gold cuff links in them. While we were all gathering around Big Jim and also watching the cave to see that no ghost came out, I noticed something about the shirt. I gasped out loud. There, as plain as day, right on the back of the white shirt, was a crooked bit of needlework, in the exact spot where my Mom had sewed up the white shirt belonging to Old Man Paddler himself only a few days ago.

"What in the world!" I thought. "Why—*why, that's Old Man Paddler's shirt!*"

And that could mean only one thing and that was that the ghost was Old Man Paddler himself. "That's Old Man Paddler's shirt!" I exclaimed. "See there, Poetry! That's the same shirt he tore on the barbed wire fence at the graveyard last Sunday afternoon!"

"Old Man Paddler can't run that fast!" Big Jim said grimly.

We all knew that that was right. That old man couldn't even run at all—unless maybe he could if he was terribly scared. But whoever it was couldn't have been a ghost, 'cause ghosts didn't wear shirts or stumble over fallen logs. In fact, if it had been a real ghost, a log wouldn't even have been in its way. It could go through a log like a radio wave goes through a house and is still a radio wave on the other side.

Just then Poetry gasped and said, "Look, everybody! There's a pencil clipped into the pocket of the shirt—an indelible pencil!"

And there was.

Well, we had to do something. You couldn't stand around at a time like that. We decided to go inside, maybe, if we weren't too scared.

Big Jim asked, "Anybody want to go home?" He looked around at Dragonfly and us, and Dragonfly said with a stutter, "I—I want to, but I—w-w-won't!" And I say, we all wanted to, but wouldn't.

"All right, everybody!" Big Jim gave the word. "When he comes out, *grab* him! And look out for smashed noses!"

I couldn't believe it. We were going to go right into the enemy's mouth. *We were going to go inside that cave!*

13

First Big Jim hollered back inside, and his voice sounded very fierce, "Come out of there, whoever you are! We'll give you until we count ten, and then we're coming in!"

All we heard in reply was a weird echo which came floating back like a screech owl's voice across the hills. *"Count ten,"* the echo said.

You see, we all had most our clothes in that cave, and some of us had our watches and knives and other things of value, so we had to go in, and I certainly didn't want to go home and go in our unlocked back door and sleep in any old nice, warm, safe bed.

Then Big Jim started to count very loud: *"One, two, three, four, five, six, seven, eight, nine, TEN!"*

We waited, and no ghost came out and there wasn't any answer. So Big Jim gave the order: "Follow Circus and me!" With that, he and Circus, with two flashlights making a white path for them, stooped low, shot the lights inside and looked in while we waited, all holding our breaths and holding also to some sticks and clubs which we'd found close by.

"It's empty," Big Jim turned to us and said, and so did Circus.

Pretty soon, in we went, and sure enough, there wasn't a thing inside except the rock walls, and our blankets and pillows and clothes and the two lonely candles looking like a couple of stalagmites standing on their shelves, with no stalactites reaching down from above.

And now what to do! The ghost or whoever or whatever it was was gone or somewhere, so we either had to give up and go to sleep or just go to sleep. We looked funny, felt crazy and scared and disappointed. If we hadn't had the shirt we wouldn't maybe have believed it, but we had the shirt and it was absolutely Old Man Paddler's.

Big Jim called us to order then and said, "I may as well tell you, to relieve your mind, that it wasn't a ghost!"

"It was too," I said. "It went in this cave, didn't it?"

"Anybody see it come in here except Dragonfly?" Circus asked.

"*I* did," I said, "with my own eyes—I think."

"Well, it isn't here now. Anybody know who it was?" Big Jim said again. "If not, we'll let it go and get some sleep."

"I s-saw it come in here headfirst," Dragonfly said fiercely. "I knew there was going to be a ghost 'cause a black cat—"

"Order!" Big Jim demanded again, and there was.

"Listen—what was *that!*" Dragonfly exclaimed. We'd all heard it. It was the sound of somebody coming.

Then as plain as day and even plainer, we heard footsteps coming toward us from somewhere. It sounded like something was coming from behind the walls, or else it was already inside and walking around unseen right among us or maybe even walking on the ceiling upside down. If it *was* a ghost or if there was any such thing as a ghost, it could do that.

I looked at Big Jim and I saw for the first time he was afraid, so I let myself be that too, without being ashamed of it.

Nearer and nearer, louder and louder came those footsteps—from somewhere behind the walls, it still sounded like—and then they stopped, so close beside me and behind me and in front of me, that I thought I could have reached out and touched who or whatever it was. I wished I'd hurry up and wake up 'cause it was the craziest dream I'd ever had, I thought.

And then all of a sudden, there in front of us,

crawling into the mouth of the cave, was an old man with white hair and long white whiskers. He had a cane and a yardstick in one hand and a long flashlight in the other, and it was Old Man Paddler himself.

It couldn't be, and yet it was.

"Good evening, everybody! May I come into your house?"

The minute I heard his voice I knew it was actually him and that I wasn't in a dream.

"I'm sorry to disturb your night's rest this way, but it's a long way home around the old wagon trail, so I decided to take a short cut. I guess I'd better rest a bit first. I'm pretty tired. Had a little business to do in town, stopped a little while in the old cemetery there at my wife's grave. I guess I must have gone to sleep there—anyway, something woke me up."

While the old man was talking and his whiskers were bobbing up and down in the light of the candles which we'd already lit, I was looking at his gray shirt which he certainly had on, and I knew the ghost hadn't been Old Man Paddler.

He shivered then and said, "It's cold in here. Ah—" He stopped and I could see from his eyes that he had an idea, and was going to spring it on us.

"Listen," he said, "I've something very important to talk to you boys about. If you'll gather up your blankets and clothes and follow me—"

With that the old man sidled over to a corner of the cave where there was a rocky ledge and gave it a little push, and say! That rock moved! *Moved!* And there as plain as candlelight could make it, was a hole leading back into the hill somewhere.

"What in the world?" different ones of us cried in absolute astonishment.

The old man turned around to us and said, "There used to be a little underground stream coming through here and flowing out into Sugar Creek. The other end, I just discovered this week, is in my own cellar. Follow me, and I'll show you. Bring your stuff along and sleep in my cabin. I'll make you some sassafras tea to warm you up a bit. You're all shivering with the cold," he finished, which we were.

Well, things were beginning to make sense—all except the white torn shirt.

Suddenly Big Jim said, "Look, Mr. Paddler! Is this your shirt?" He held out the shirt all torn to shreds toward the old man, who looked at it. He started like somebody had stuck him with a pin or something.

"Where did you *get* that?"

"I just tore it off Bob Till ten minutes ago," Big Jim said, and that made me start and all the rest of us also.

For a minute there was silence, that is, until we heard a door slam faraway somewhere. Poetry looked at me quick and I at him and all of a sudden we knew that we had known something a long time, and that was that there was a door in the basement of Old Man Paddler's cabin at the other end of the tunnel into whose jaws we were looking right that very minute.

Well, that was the beginning of the end of this story, which is almost too long now.

"Bob Till," Old Man Paddler said to us all, "has been staying at my cabin this week, while I've been trying to make arrangements to have the law give him still another chance, without making him go to the reformatory. I don't want him to go there, if I can help it. I keep thinking what if it was my William or one of my other sons who is dead now. I think if I can teach him a few things which his father should have taught him a long time ago, we can make a decent citizen of him, and maybe he can become a Christian. A boy has to *hear* the gospel, you know, before he can be saved."

There was more which Old Man Paddler said, but that is enough for you to know.

Say, we gathered up our clothes, putting most of

124

them on, and with our blankets and pillows and I with my sleeping bag, went through that dark hole in the side of the hill, and followed that old man back and back, winding and winding, stooping here and there, and passing little piles of dirt and rock which Old Man Paddler and Bob had made when they had had to dig through a place that was too small for a man or boy to go through.

Pretty soon we came to a new door and sure enough, we were in Old Man Paddler's basement, and then we were up in his fine, neat old cabin, saving ourselves a mile of walking.

"Boy, that will save him a lot of walking when he has to go to town, won't it?" Poetry said to me, puffing hard, and always glad of anything that would save walking or working.

"It'll be especially good next winter," the old man said, having heard what Poetry said, as he busied himself lighting the fire in his stove to make some sassafras tea for us, to get the shivers out of us.

Well, as I said, that was the beginning of the end of this story about the Sugar Creek Gang in School, most of the important things in this book not happening in school, but while we were having to go to school that fall anyway.

Right that minute I heard somebody in Old Man

Paddler's upstairs coughing a little like he had a cold, and it sounded like a boy's cough.

"That's Bob Till," Old Man Paddler said. "I've been taking care of him. Poor fellow, he hasn't even had enough clothes of his own, so I've been letting him wear some of mine. I suppose that's where that white shirt came from. He'd been in the cemetery doing a little cleaning up around my sons' graves. He was afraid to do it in the daytime, so I let him go at night. He's still got a sense of shame, you know, like most boys have, if you can dig deep enough to find it, or maybe if almighty God can get a chance to put it into him," the old man explained.

So we slept in the old man's cabin and different things happened which you won't get to hear about right now. But this much you ought to know: The next Monday morning when the seventeen pupils of the Sugar Creek School, No. 9, were all sitting in their seats studying or supposed to be studying, all of a sudden Big Jim raised his hand. Miss Lilly looked at him and nodded, and he motioned for her to come to his desk, which she did.

I was trying to find out what that same Mr. Brown, who had had trouble with his wool and sheep and his bank account and his lumber bill, was going to do about his *coal* bill, so it was easy for me to look up and watch and listen to see what was going on in Big Jim's mind.

And do you know what? He said to Miss Lilly—and his voice was very clear and like a man's—"The Sugar Creek Gang is ready now to sign that paper, if we may, please."

And so was all the rest of the school.

Well, this is the end. I really don't know whether there could be anything as important happen to the Sugar Creek Gang as I've just written to you about, but if anything does happen, I'll take plenty of time out to tell you about it. In fact, I can almost feel that something *is* going to happen, 'cause that very afternoon, after school was out and I was on my way home, I had to go past Circus' house for something, and his dad's big hunting dogs, with their long noses and also their long voices, had something up a tree and were making plenty of dog noise.

"Hello there, Bill Collins," Circus' dad's husky voice called to me. "Fall is almost here, and I've planned a hunting trip some dark, drizzling night, and I'd like all the Sugar Creek Gang to go along. I saw coon tracks along the mouth of the branch this morning."

I went on home, thinking about that hunting trip and wishing my parents would let me go. It would be fun to go hunting along with the gang, walking in the shadows of the lantern through the dark woods and along Sugar Creek, and hear the long-tongued bawling of the hounds; and we might even catch—well, 'most anything.

Moody Press, a ministry of the Moody Bible Institute, is designed for education, evangelization and edification. If we may assist you in knowing more about Christ and the Christian life, please write us without obligation to:

Moody Press, c/o MLM, Chicago, Illinois 60610.